A Lyon to Die For

The Lyon's Den Connected World

E.L. Johnson

ARE YOU SIGNED UP FOR DRAGONBLADE'S BLOG?

You'll get the latest news and information on exclusive giveaways, exclusive excerpts, coming releases, sales, free books, cover reveals and more.

Check out our complete list of authors, too!

No spam, no junk. That's a promise!

Sign Up Here

www.dragonbladepublishing.com

Dearest Reader;

Thank you for your support of a small press. At Dragonblade Publishing, we strive to bring you the highest quality Historical Romance from some of the best authors in the business. Without your support, there is no 'us', so we sincerely hope you adore these stories and find some new favorite authors along the way.

Happy Reading!

CEO, Dragonblade Publishing

Additional Dragonblade books by Author E.L. Johnson

The Perfect Poison Murders
The Strangled Servant (Book 1)
The Poisoned Clergyman (Book 2)
The Mistress Murders (Book 3)
The Deadly Debutante (Book 4)
The Betrayed Bride (Book 5)

The Lyon's Den Series
The Lyon and the Bluestocking
A Lyon to Die For

Other Lyon's Den Books

CHAPTER ONE

London 1815

E MMELINE HARCOURT GENTLY closed the window to her sister-in-law's millinery shop with a snap. She tutted at the chill wind that whispered inside Harcourt's Hats. Rain gently pattered down outside. Tucked away on a side street connected to New Bond Street, Emmeline peered out the solid glass windows as the rain properly came down, dousing nearby people in seconds.

That was British weather, she supposed. Rain one moment and then sunny skies the next. She felt for the poor souls that struggled by without an umbrella.

It was September, past the rainy season, and yet since she had relocated to London from Bedford, she had already gotten drenched enough times in sudden downpours to know that rainy London deserved its reputation. As such, she was now prepared and carried a small parasol that bore oilskin instead of silk or taffeta. But it was a bit heavy and cumbersome.

She watched as one such woman dressed in a dark cloak trudged through the streets, gripping her cloak tightly around her. Emmeline's heart went out to her, for she was clearly ill-prepared for the rain. The lady walked with purpose, her head and black bonnet faced down, but she was still getting pelted by the rain that had picked up.

Emmeline watched as a carriage passed by and its wheels splattered water and mud on the woman. If that weren't enough, a malicious stray wind ripped her black straw bonnet and veil off her head, sending them sailing down the street. The woman turned, her mouth an open *o* of surprise, and she gritted her teeth.

Emmeline was hurrying outside before she realized what she was doing, umbrella in hand.

Her sister-in-law called, "Emmy, what are you...?"

The doorbell rang in her wake as she darted into the wet air. Emmeline opened the umbrella and hurried to the woman, holding it over her. "Pardon me, ma'am. Won't you come inside?"

The woman, her middle-aged face plastered with wet hair, looked at her. "I beg your pardon?" Then, a beat later, she said, "Yes. I need a new veil."

Emmeline led her inside the shop, the bell ringing as they entered. Emmeline lowered the umbrella and shut the door behind them.

"Ugh. What monstrous weather. I love London, and yet I hate it in equal measure sometimes," the woman said.

Emmeline smiled and closed the umbrella, leaning it in a small stand by the door.

"A useful contraption, that. I'd forgotten mine," the woman said. "Actually, that's not true. I'd purposely left it at my house, thinking it was a beautiful day. And it was, until about ten minutes ago. Serves me right to leave the house without one."

Emmeline smiled again. "I saw what happened. Are you all right?"

"Just a bit wet, I suppose. Nothing a cup of tea and a hot bath won't fix." The woman looked around the shop. "I've never been in here before."

Her sister-in-law swooped down on the potential customer. "Hello, we are Harcourt's Hats. I am Mrs. Harcourt. I can see you are without a hat. Can I interest you in a bonnet? We have a nice selection for the—"

The woman glanced at Mrs. Harcourt. "This young lady was showing me around." She turned to Emmeline. "If you might continue?"

Emmeline blinked. "Yes, of course." She first picked up a stray bolt of cotton fabric near the woman and handed it to her. "For your face."

"Thank you." The older woman wiped her face and patted her damp hair, drying herself off. She handed it back. "Show me your hats and veils," she commanded.

Emmeline took her around the shop and stepped back. In her mind, it wasn't just a shop. It was almost a display, like what one would see at a grand bazaar or a great exhibition.

Their shop sold hats, but that was the least of it, Emmeline thought. They specialized in hats, but also sold gloves, parasols, feathers, and miniature flowers for the enterprising at-home hat maker.

She brought the newcomer by an array of caps, demonstrating how each one was different from the next. One was of a bell shape made of delicate white crêpe, trimmed with fake yellow flowers.

On the next table perched turbans, such as one with three bands against the white crêpe, with red roses dotting the front. Emmeline gently touched a Venetian-style bonnet, made of straw and trimmed with miniature flowers, with the silken ribbon fastened with a bow. She caressed the stiff folds of her favorite, a Neapolitan bonnet, constructed of leghorn and with a curved round bill that fitted almost like a soft shell around the face, but was fashioned in a burnished gold silk material that caught the light. The fact that it too had a matching ribbon and miniature pink flowers was almost secondary. As a beam of sunlight shone through the windows through the fading rain, it lit up the hat, making it shine and gleam like a piece of fine jewelry or pirate gold.

"How beautiful," the woman murmured, touching it. She picked it up. "What a fetching hat." She set it down.

The woman kept by her side, asking questions about this cap, or that bonnet. She seemed particularly interested in the selection of black bonnets with veils, admiring one dressed with Norwich crêpe. "Your shop is new, I take it."

"Yes. We have lately come from Bedfordshire."

"And you are new to town, are you not?"

"Yes, we've opened a little over a month ago." And had met no one, hardly even their neighbors. Despite their being in London these five years past, they had only recently discovered a lease to the shop and spent the past months setting it up. But that left little time for socializing. For all that she enjoyed the sights and sounds of London, living in their little townhouse in Cheapside, they hardly knew a soul and spent most evenings indoors.

The woman purchased a fashionable cap of black crêpe with a gauze overlay, trimmed with a smart blue wreath and miniature bows. As she paid for her purchase, she asked, "Do you and your mother make the hats yourselves?"

"What my sister-in-law and I don't make ourselves, we order in the latest fashions from Paris, and the ladies' magazines, so we're never out of style. Was there something you wanted to order?"

"No, I'm fine." The lady also bought a hat of black satin and ostrich feathers that swooped gallantly over the bill, offering shade with a bit of a flounce. "May I wear this out?"

"It is your hat. Of course," Emmeline said, passing it to her. She helped the woman fix it to her hair and used a strong hat pin to set it in place amongst her damp tresses and new veil.

"You have been by my side so long, I feel guilty for having kept you away from your duties," the lady said.

Emmeline smiled at her, very aware that they stood alone in the

4

shop, aside from her sister-in-law.

"I shall mention your shop to my friends. What is your name, girl?"

"Emmeline Harcourt. It's a pleasure to meet you, Mrs...."

"Dove-Lyon. I run a small establishment on Cleveland Row. Why not call and join me this evening for a small party I am having? Bring your sister-in-law along too." She glanced at Emmeline, taking in her soft blonde hair pinned back in an industrious bun, her striped dress, cut with a high neck for propriety, down to her shined black shoes. "You make a very fetching portrait. You are single, are you not?"

Emmeline's eyebrows rose at the woman's forwardness. They had just been introduced and now she was asking her about her marital status? What cheek.

"Forgive my directness, Miss Harcourt. It is that I find myself at a loss for company this evening, and you have cheered me up very well. Do say you'll come along to dinner." She pressed Emmeline's hand with her black gloved one.

"We would be delighted," Charlotte said.

Mrs. Dove-Lyon said, "Then it's settled. Call on me at five." She handed Emmeline her card, checked her reflection of her new hat and veil in a small looking glass, and took her second hat out in a charming striped box, the hanging bell ringing behind her.

"Well, what an interesting woman. What do you make of her?" Charlotte asked. "A curious sort of personality. And so affable, to invite us to dinner. Very kind."

"So odd. We'd just met, and she was asking about whether I was single."

"You know these eccentric women. Did you see the way she was dressed? All that lace. And those jet buttons, the way they caught the light. Stunning."

"Charlotte?"

"She's just trying to do right by you, is all. She can see we are new to town and wants to help introduce us to company. It's very kind of her. Now, what shall we wear to dinner?"

Emmeline laughed. She had learned from her mother to always aim to be the best-dressed woman in the room, or if she could not afford it, then at least wear the finest hat for any occasion.

The day passed quietly. One or two people came into the shop but only bought umbrellas. A few men walked by, peering in the windows without coming in, which rather made Emmeline feel on display.

One man walked inside, kicking the door open with a bang. The bell clanged angrily, as if announcing the arrival of a feuding knight.

His steps were loud in the quiet shop, and he sneered at the arrangements of hats, parasols, gloves, and lace. His gaze alighted on Charlotte and Emmeline, and he looked them up and down, causing Emmeline to grit her teeth. To look at a woman was no crime, but to leer in such an open manner bordered on disrespect.

Charlotte approached him with a ready smile. "Hello. Welcome to our shop. Can I help you find anything?"

"No." The man crossed his arms over his chest. He was a powerfully built man, barrel-chested, with a piggish glint in his eyes. "Are you aware of the history of this street?"

"I beg your pardon?"

"This street has some of the finest shops in all of London. They are owned by men. They cater to men. They do not..." he looked at the nearest display, "sell lace."

"I was unaware of that," Charlotte said reasonably.

"When I approved the lease of this shop, I was under the impression it was to be a milliner."

"It is."

"For men. I approved the lease to Mr. Harcourt. Where is he?"

Emmeline didn't like where this was going. She marched up as Charlotte quailed, her hands darting to her black gown.

"He is..."

"Where's the owner?" the man barked.

"Mr. Harcourt is dead. I am his wife. When he died, the ownership passed to me, as per his will," Charlotte said quietly. "Can I help you w—"

"Hah! Don't you know this isn't a street for women's millinery? Where's the man of the establishment? If not your husband, then find someone else. A man I can talk to, dear."

Charlotte balked and unconsciously took a step back. The man smiled, and Emmeline stood in his way. "There is no man of the establishment. This is our shop."

He looked down at her, or rather, her bosom. He stared for a few seconds, then slowly raised his eyes to her face. "I see. I normally don't approve of female proprietors in my street, but perhaps we might come to some arrangement..."

Emmeline felt outraged. Her voice shook. "Please leave before I call the constabulary."

"What for? I'm doing nothing wrong. This is my property." His beady eyes glared down at her.

"You're being a nuisance, and the lease belongs to us. Get out," Emmeline said.

"I'd do what the lady says, Mr. Bryant," a low voice said behind her.

She whirled around. There stood a man she'd never seen before. She'd been so distracted by Mr. Bryant, she'd never even heard him come in, but the very sight of him made her pause. He was tall, with wavy brown hair that threatened to fall around his eyes. He had bushy thick eyebrows and skin that leaned toward paleness, a bullish nose, and a square jaw with a hint of fuzz around the chin. His blue-gray eyes pierced her, and he smelled intoxicating.

Emmeline blinked and stepped back. She had no time for this. There was a bully she had to face. She whirled back around.

Mr. Bryant's mouth curled into a sneer. "Whittaker? I should've known you'd be there. Couldn't help but sniff around the ladies, eh?"

"You would know, Bryant. How is our favorite actress?"

Mr. Bryant's sneering mouth withered. "My dear wife is fine. I would say she sends her love, but I'd be lying. I keep her too busy to think of any other man." He smirked.

Emmeline saw Mr. Whittaker's hands curl into fists, and she feared for the safety of her shop's goods. "Gentlemen, if you would take this outside…"

The men looked at her, remembering where they were.

She glared at them, not budging, when the door opened and a short man entered, dripping wet, in a damp gray suit. "Excuse me, I'm looking for a hat for my… oh, am I interrupting?"

"No, this man was just leaving," Emmeline said, staring into the bully's eyes.

Mr. Bryant grinned. "Right you are. But I'll be back. Make no mistake, your lease will not be renewed. This is no place for a woman's shop." He turned and knocked over a display of gloves, sending them flying to the floor. He trod on one. "First Whittaker and now you. Banfield, what are you doing here? Come to eye the ladies too, eh? Playing the happy widower? They won't be interested." He shoved past the short man and walked out, the bell ringing angrily in his wake.

Emmeline's shoulders drooped as if she'd just fought in a boxing ring. She let out a breath she didn't realize she'd been holding. She looked at the stranger he'd addressed as Whittaker. "That was kind of you to intervene, but I didn't need your help."

The man's pleasant expression turned into a frown. "Is that how you say 'thank you' where you're from?"

"I was dealing with him fine on my own."

"Of course you were. You must not be from around here. Do they teach manners outside of London?" Mr. Whittaker asked.

She bristled. "Are all gentlemen so presumptuous where you're from?"

"I was taught that a gentleman should defend a woman when she is threatened." He glared at her.

"As I said, I did not need your help." She put her hands on her hips.

"Has anyone ever told you that your sales technique needs improvement?"

"No. You would be the first." She glared into his blue-gray eyes, mentally cursing him for being so attractive.

"Emmeline, really. He was just being polite," Charlotte said. "Thank you, sir. That was very kind of you."

The man touched his hat and walked out, bypassing the mess of gloves on the floor.

"My word, what a horrid man. I'm glad Mr. Bryant is gone," Charlotte said, walking toward the disturbed display.

"Let me help," the new man said, rushing forward to pick up the gloves. "I say, this is a new shop, isn't it?"

"We just opened a month ago," Charlotte said, picking up a pair of gloves and dusting them off.

"Jolly good. Nice sort of shop you've got here." The man said, looking around. "That's Logan Bryant whom you met earlier. He owns most of the shops around here. I'm Charles Banfield. I run a flower shop just across the way." He patted a small, dainty flower in his buttonhole above his pocket and gave her a shy smile.

Charlotte blushed prettily and curtsied to him. "Charlotte Harcourt. This is my sister-in-law, Emmeline."

"Pleasure to meet you both. Don't worry about Mr. Bryant, he likes to throw his weight around, but he is more bark than bite."

"I hope so," Charlotte said, fretting.

"You are in mourning?" Mr. Banfield said, noting her black clothing.

"Yes. We had just moved to London and my husband died in a carriage accident. We've been here a few years and would have canceled the lease, but when I saw he'd left the shop to me, I thought he'd want me to carry on. So here we are," Charlotte said.

Emmeline looked at her sister-in-law with fondness. She was tall and slim, with fair blond hair the color of ash, with slivers of silver mixing in. Emmeline loved Charlotte like she was her own sister and respected her relation's quiet strength.

"And are you going out into society much?" he asked.

"Not much. But I suppose we will. Why just this evening, we were invited to join a Mrs. Dove-Lyon for dinner."

Mr. Banfield coughed. "Mrs. Dove-Lyon? Of the Lyon's Den?"

"I beg your pardon?" Charlotte asked, "What den?"

"What lions?" Emmeline asked.

Mr. Banfield swallowed and fussed over the miniature flower in his breast pocket that drooped. He said, "Mrs. Dove-Lyon is indeed a kind and pleasant woman. But her reputation is, well…"

Charlotte's eyebrows rose. "Sir?"

He said in a hushed voice, "She runs a gambling den in her home. Invite only. If you are invited to join her, I suspect you will get a chance to inspect her institution."

"My word. A gambling den?"

"Yes. I have um… seen it before. Once or twice. Perhaps I might see you there," he said.

"I don't approve of gambling. But… It would make the evening so much more pleasant if I had someone to talk to," Charlotte said.

Emmeline snorted. Her sister-in-law had forgotten she was there. She left them to talk and began to tidy up the displays.

"Who was that man? The other one," Charlotte asked Mr. Banfield.

"Oh, him? That's Horatio Whittaker."

"Horatio? What a funny name."

"Yes. He owns a shop on this street too. Well. To be honest, he owns my shop, as a matter of fact. I keep things running day to day."

Emmeline stifled a groan. There would be no avoiding seeing

them on a regular basis if they also were shopkeepers on the same street.

"He seemed very kind," Charlotte said.

"He can be a trifle proud, but he's a good enough chap." The young man dusted his hands and brushed off his trousers. "Well, I should be going. Do call on me sometime. I'd be happy to arrange an order of flowers for your hats."

"Oh, that would be excellent. Do come back soon." Charlotte curtsied to the man's bow and smiled as he left. She turned to Emmeline. "Such a kind gentleman. And he works with flowers, we're sure to get a good deal on them. Don't you think?"

Emmeline nodded. "Trust you to make friends as soon as we arrive."

"I prefer honey to vinegar. Besides, I didn't see you charming anyone."

"We're in business. I don't need to charm."

"Maybe not, but you don't need to make enemies either. What was your problem with Mr. Whittaker? He seemed like he was trying to do us a kindness."

"He involved himself in our business when there was no need to. I was handling it fine."

"You were, but I'd never say no to a bit of help," Charlotte said. "Especially from one so handsome as Mr. Whittaker."

"I didn't notice." Emmeline sniffed and turned her back.

"Hah!"

CHAPTER TWO

T HAT EVENING AFTER they closed the shop, the women returned to their townhouse and dressed for dinner. Charlotte wore a mourning dress of black tinged with mauve, while Emmeline put on an evening dress of pink trimmed with white lace. Their maids arranged their hair in fetching and comely styles, and once bedecked with jewelry and cloaks of black and aubergine, they took a carriage to Mrs. Dove-Lyon's home at Cleveland Row.

They were met at a side entrance and ushered into a building lit by lanterns outside. Inside was well lit with candles that offered a warm golden glow. They met Mrs. Dove-Lyon, who wore a smart black veil over an evening dress of black satin, and joined a grand table of well-dressed men and women for dinner. But much to Emmeline's dismay, she was seated next to a familiar face.

Mr. Whittaker wore a stiff white cravat, charcoal gray suit, and silvery waistcoat. His dark hair was combed and framed his square face and firm jaw perfectly. It annoyed her to see him looking so perfect. He smelled good, too, which only irked her further. He smelled of rich red wine, cologne, and wood smoke, as if he'd just come from outside. He raised an eyebrow as she sat beside him.

She did her best to ignore him, and once they were all seated, Mrs. Dove-Lyon made introductions. At her mentioning Mr. Whittaker, they both looked away. "Oh, I see you know each other," Mrs. Dove-Lyon said.

"We met earlier," Mr. Whittaker said.

"Excellent." Mrs. Dove-Lyon kept the conversation light and cheerful while the group dined on a rich soup.

"What are you doing here, Miss Harcourt?" he asked quietly.

"Eating dinner. What does it look like?"

"I mean, why are you here? This dinner. This place. You don't belong here. You do know what it is, don't you?"

She disliked his tone. "What do you mean? Charlotte and I were invited."

His mouth half quirked in a smile.

"What?" she asked.

"The only reason Mrs. Dove-Lyon invites people here is to make connections."

"And lo and behold, it's a dinner party. It seems to be a perfectly reasonable way to meet new people," she said.

He turned to her. "Are you really that naive?"

"Are you always so rude to people at dinner?" she asked.

He blinked. "Only those who deserve it."

"And what I have done to earn your ire? After a long day at the shop, where my sister-in-law and I dealt with some very unfriendly customers, we accepted an invitation to dinner. It was pleasant up until now."

He grunted and drank some wine. "I find your willful obliviousness to be annoying."

"I find your rudeness annoying. How can I possibly have offended by accepting a dinner invitation?" She frowned at him.

"Do you really not know?"

"Perhaps I am not so *willfully* oblivious as you may think," she said.

He set down his wine glass and cut savagely into the roast pigeon on his plate, his knife screeching across the china. "The Lyon's Den has a certain reputation. The men and women come here to gamble and place wagers, but also to meet and... socialize."

She blinked. "It sounds a bit unorthodox, but hardly improper."

Mr. Whittaker smiled at his food as he cut into the pigeon, his knife scoring the crispy skin. "It is no better than a marriage mart, Miss Harcourt. But then, you would have no need of that, would you?"

She glanced at him. "The men and women come here to meet..."

"With an eye toward marriage, yes. Now do you see why I find your presence here so unsettling?"

"No. We were under the impression this was a dinner party and nothing else. Do you think she will try to fix up my sister-in-law and me?"

"Mrs. Dove-Lyon is an expert in matters of the heart. She may have done so already. But I pity the man who is destined for your company."

Her head snapped toward him as if he'd struck her. "That was rude."

"I thought a woman like you appreciated honesty."

"I do, but I like a bit of common courtesy as well. A bit of politeness goes a long way," she said with a hard tone. Her face felt hot, as she saw more than one person's eyes on her. Sipping her wine, she said in a hushed voice, "I fail to see why you seek to spar with me, especially when I notice you have no young lady hanging on your every word. Is it perhaps because your style of conversation puts off more women than it attracts?"

He snorted and mildly paid attention to the other diners, particularly a man who described the games of faro and hazard taking place in the Den. His attention was then grabbed by a pretty blonde woman sat across from him, who gave him a demure smile, revealing salad in her teeth. He looked away, disgusted.

"Then tell me why it is that *you* are here. Are you on the hunt for the future Mrs. Whittaker?" she asked.

"Hardly."

"It is the wine, perhaps. Or the fine dinners."

He ignored her. "It's certainly not the company."

She put down her wine glass and glared at him, her mouth pursed in a frown. She whispered, "Is it that you disapprove of our being here, considering we are in trade?"

"Not at all. Unlike some, I have no problem with a woman in business."

She eyed him. "I heard that you run a shop on New Bond Street."

He barely acknowledged it and drank more wine. "I own one, but I never said I run it," he said with disdain, as if to work was unseemly.

"My word, perhaps that's it. You think my hat shop will ruin the flower shop you have Mr. Banfield run, is that it?" She said, "We do use flowers often, I must admit."

He almost spat out his wine.

"What were you doing in our shop earlier? Lurking around to see what we were up to?" she asked.

"No. I, too, came and wanted to say hello to the new owners. Welcome you to the street."

She sat back in her seat, glancing at him.

"What?"

"I'm waiting," she said.

"For what?"

"My welcome."

He stabbed a forkful of pigeon. "That moment has passed."

"Excuse me, but I think I heard you mention earlier. Do you really own a shop?" A pretty redhead next to him started a conversation and Emmeline rolled her eyes as he happily engaged the woman in discussion for the rest of the meal.

They dined on roast pigeon with wild garlic and sage, red wine, and plum fruit tarts for dessert.

Once dinner ended, they were quick to part ways, for which Emmeline felt grateful.

As she stood by the gambling tables and observed people lose at faro and whist, Emmeline watched as Mr. Whittaker chatted gaily with the redheaded young woman, who stuck close to his side. But strangely enough, he excused himself and found his way over to her.

"Finally enjoying the company?" she asked.

He sniffed. "Tolerable. Break any men's hearts?"

"Not yet. You seem to have made a new friend," she pointed out.

"I have." He glanced back at the young woman who stood watching him. "Her breath smells. And she has food stuck in her teeth."

Emmeline smiled. "Why would you tell me such a thing? That's not very gallant."

"I never said I was. I was only commenting on the company."

She raised an eyebrow. "I wonder if the young lady feels the same way."

He shrugged. "She spoke of little beyond an interest in how many shops I own, and where she might buy a good hat." He grunted. "I told her to visit your shop."

"That is very kind of you," she said.

He stared at her. "Are you feeling all right?"

"Yes, why?"

"You were polite," he said.

Emmeline laughed. "You are teasing me."

"Not at all. You are the one laughing, I might add," he said.

"Touché."

He whisked two glasses of wine from a nearby servant and handed one to her. They stood by as Charlotte entered the room. Even in a dress of black and mauve, she was a pretty sight, and it made Emmeline sigh and wish for an ounce of her natural beauty.

Charlotte had a stunning presence, with long blonde hair that, even pinned up, left fair tendrils around her heart-shaped face that was a touch pale. She had a long slim body, and when she moved it was with a natural grace, like that of a dancer.

But her expression was cold and haunted, as if she feared to even gaze into the eyes of a man. She walked through the room, completely unaware of the longing gazes she attracted from the men, and the envious looks she earned from the women. In the right color, she would be exceedingly beautiful, but she wore a step away from deep mourning colors, and it was clear to all present that she was not inclined to invite attention.

"I'd better go to my sister-in-law," Emmeline said.

But it was a matter of seconds before Charlotte was met by a servant, who asked her a question. She shook her head and walked on, searching for someone.

Emmeline met her, and said, "Is everything all right?"

"Yes, I was looking for you."

"What did the servant want?"

Charlotte gave her head a minute shake. "He said a gentleman wished to be introduced to me."

"But you said no."

"Of course I did. I'm a widow." She blinked and looked at Emmeline. "It would be wrong to encourage attention."

"But you might make new acquaintances. We are new here. To refuse might be considered rude."

Charlotte shrugged and looked over Emmeline's shoulder. "Oh, hello, Mr. Whittaker. Did you enjoy dinner?"

"Mrs. Harcourt. Yes, the roast pigeon and jam tarts were excellent. How are you?"

"Well enough." She looked around the room. "I think I am overly warm. Let us go upstairs, Emmy."

"Emmy?" Mr. Whittaker repeated.

Charlotte smiled as Emmeline turned pink. "My little affectionate name for my sister-in-law. Do excuse us, Mr. Whittaker." Charlotte set aside Emmeline's drink, took her hand, and whisked her away, ignoring the servants and men who watched and looked keen to strike up a conversation.

"Charlotte, where are you taking us?" Emmeline asked.

"Away from here." Her shoulders hunched slightly and took on a hunted air. "I am too warm down here with all these people." She led Emmeline across the room, and up a spiral staircase that led to an observation balcony and a series of gambling rooms and parlors just for women.

Once they were safely ensconced in one of the private rooms, away from the general view of the guests, Charlotte sat on a plush sofa bedecked with pink cushions and dark black wooden framing, and let out a small sigh of relief.

"Charlotte, are you all right?"

"Yes, now that we're away from all those people. I could feel them staring. I… did not like it at all. I felt so observed, like a specimen in a museum." She gave a slight shiver.

Better than to be overlooked as insignificant, Emmeline thought, and dismissed the notion just as easily. She felt a pang of jealousy over her relative's beauty but banished the thought out of concern for her well-being. "What can I do?"

"Nothing. Can we go?" Charlotte asked.

"Of course. I'll ask a servant to call us a hackney." She rose to fetch a servant, when she bumped into Mrs. Dove-Lyon.

"Is your sister-in-law all right? She looked pale and you left the room so suddenly," Mrs. Dove-Lyon said.

"She's fine, but I need to take her home. I need to call us a carriage and fetch our cloaks." She turned to Mrs. Dove-Lyon. "Thank you for the dinner. Your institution is… most entertaining."

Mrs. Dove-Lyon smiled at this attempt at diplomacy. "You are welcome to call at any time." She raised a hand and in seconds, a servant attended them. Once the order had been placed for a carriage and their things, they left, but not without earning a thoughtful look from their hostess.

It was funny, Emmeline reflected during the carriage ride back to Cheapside, how despite Charlotte being twenty-seven years to her twenty-two, she felt like the older of the two. Since Charlotte had entered their family, she had felt like a sister, if she'd ever had one. And since her brother's death five years ago, they had become closer still, as they grieved and gradually resumed life without him.

"We could always move back to Bedfordshire," Emmeline said in the quiet of the carriage.

Charlotte pulled her black cloak around her more tightly. "Don't be ridiculous. There's no need. And we have the shop."

"But Charlotte…"

"No. Do not even think it. I have no wish to go back there and be the subject of the family's pitying looks, and I daresay you do not wish so either." Her voice held a pointed note, and her sharp eyes sought out Emmeline's.

Emmeline looked down. "No."

"Then let's speak no more of the matter."

But as the carriage bumped and jolted, the noise of the horse's hooves clattering against the cobblestone streets of London, Emmeline wondered, not for the first time, if something ought to change in her life. Was this all she was meant for, spending her days in the shop and trading verbal barbs with snooty gentlemen, or annoying her dear sister-in-law?

The next day Charlotte was feeling poorly and stayed at home. Emmeline opened the shop herself, sold a few hats and sets of gloves, and took a few orders, when the bell over the door rang, announcing the arrival of Mrs. Dove-Lyon.

"Hello, what a pleasure to see you again."

Mrs. Dove-Lyon smiled and strode in, wearing one of the two new black hats she had purchased there. It looked very fetching with the black, gauzy veil that hid her face, giving her an air of mystery. She looked around the shop and approached Emmeline. "Good morning."

"Have you come looking for another hat? A set of gloves perhaps, or a parasol?"

"No, not this time. I've come to see you."

"Oh?"

Mrs. Dove-Lyon smiled enigmatically and clasped her hands. "I couldn't help but hear how a certain gentleman wished to be introduced to your sister, and she refused the connection."

"Ah." Emmeline blushed a little. "You see, she wasn't feeling well and—"

Mrs. Dove-Lyon held up a gloved hand. "I quite understand. She is a widow, and not yet ready to socialize again. But... that gentleman was a man of some standing, and he was, I regret to say, offended."

"Oh no." Emmeline's hand went to her mouth. "I'm sorry to hear that."

"Yes. Be that as it may, we made our apologies and smoothed over the matter. But I have little doubt that he will not be the last who attempts to get to know your sister-in-law. She is quite beautiful."

Emmeline felt a pang of envy. *She* had never been called beautiful before.

"I don't know what you have heard about my little establishment, but... I pride myself on being a good judge of character. Particularly when it comes to marriage."

Emmeline's expression was wooden.

"I wonder if perhaps your sister-in-law would care to make use of my services? I have helped many couples come together in matrimony."

Emmeline shook her head. "My sister-in-law is in mourning."

"I noticed. I'm sorry to hear of it. When did her husband pass away?"

Emmeline swallowed and looked away. "My brother died some five years ago."

A delicate eyebrow rose. "I am sorry for your loss."

"Thank you."

"With Mrs. Harcourt's pretty face, she will have no want of admirers. But she is still in mourning for him."

"Very much. I do not think she plans to stop."

"She should not stay in such deep mourning forever."

But aren't you? Emmeline thought. "It was very kind of you to invite us to dinner last night, Mrs. Dove-Lyon, thank you."

"It was my pleasure. I was glad to see you making such excellent conversation with Mr. Whittaker over dinner. Many find his conversation lacking, but I've always thought him a fine catch, for the right young lady."

Emmeline blinked. "I hadn't noticed."

Mrs. Dove-Lyon's expression suggested she didn't believe that for a moment. "Well, in any case, I wonder if you and your sister-in-law might like to partake in the entertainment at my establishment. People call it the Lyon's Den, but it is just a place where I gather my friends."

"I have heard that it is a place where men go to meet eligible women."

"Many do come for that purpose, but not all. Some go to gamble, or drink, and avoid a certain element of society that might be found in a common tavern or inn. I offer discretion. And if so desired, an opportunity for introductions." She looked Emmeline in the eyes. "You might think on this. If there was a certain gentleman who caught your eye, or your sister-in-law's, I could arrange it."

"I think we're fine. Thank you."

"As you wish." She left.

Emmeline ran the shop, and while she sold a few items with a happy smile, her mind was distracted. She wanted Charlotte to be happy, but didn't want to pressure her into too many social engagements when she wasn't ready. Still, what if Mrs. Dove-Lyon was right, and it was time? Perhaps her offer had come at an opportune moment.

That evening she went home and dined with Charlotte at the small dining table in their townhouse, the only sound being the slight clink of their cutlery against the china plates as they dined on carrots, seasoned potatoes, and a thick soup.

"What is it, Emmy? You've had a puzzled look on your face since you got home. Did something happen at the shop today?" Charlotte asked.

"Mrs. Dove-Lyon came to see me."

"Oh? Did you thank her for dinner last night?"

"Yes. But she also wanted to offer her services," Emmeline said.

"Hah. That doesn't surprise me. If she offers, most women try their hand at it, I think. If a woman is not either married or widowed between the ages of sixteen and thirty, she must be wanting a man. What poppycock," Charlotte said.

"You think so?"

"Of course. Look at me. I was perfectly happy with Anthony, and now…" Charlotte looked down at her soup. "I am perfectly happy now."

Emmeline took in the sight of Charlotte's mauve and black gauzy dress. She'd gotten so used to seeing her sister-in-law wearing black, she hadn't spared a thought for her to wear anything else. "Are you?"

That earned her a sharp look. "Don't tell me you're thinking of accepting Mrs. Dove-Lyon's offer?"

Emmeline shrugged and stirred her soup.

"Take her help for yourself if you like, but leave me out of it. I have no wish to get entangled up in someone else's schemes, especially a matchmaker who enjoys toying with people's hearts."

"I'm sure she would approach things more delicately than that," Emmeline said.

"Are you? How well do you know her? We met her only yesterday. Is that enough for you to develop a good sense of judgment of her character?" Charlotte's eyes narrowed. "Have you come so far from your time in Bedfordshire that you are now better at assessing others?"

Emmeline met her sharp gaze. "That was uncalled for."

"But necessary. Do not toy with me, Emmeline, and I will return the favor."

The women ate their soup in silence. They spent another long evening together, reading by candlelight, with Emmeline watching Charlotte reading the latest articles in a lady's magazine. Her sister-in-law sighed and put down the magazine in favor of a romance novel, where the hero stole the heroine away in the dead of night. From the way her shoulders shook with laughter at some parts, and how she sighed at others, Emmeline wondered if perhaps Charlotte was truly happy.

But later that night, Emmeline woke up to the sound of crying. She wandered down the corridor and traced the source of the sound— Charlotte's bedchamber. As she stood outside her sister-in-law's door, Emmeline's shoulders slumped. Charlotte was crying herself to sleep, and not for the first time.

Emmeline wanted to go in and hold her, but knew from past experience that Charlotte was proud and would not welcome the interruption. So she wandered back to her room, quiet in the knowledge of Charlotte's unhappiness. But as she closed her bedroom door behind her and slipped under the covers, she felt a grim determination. Something had to change.

The next day Emmeline penned a note to Mrs. Dove-Lyon and took tea with her in the afternoon. They met at the blue house on Cleveland Row, over black tea and scones, and Mrs. Dove-Lyon wore her customary mourning clothes and widow's veil. "I would like to take you up on your offer after all," Emmeline started.

Mrs. Dove-Lyon smiled and named her price.

Emmeline blinked. "That much?"

"True matchmaking is a skill, and one I am pleased to say I have in abundance. That is the price of success. If, for whatever reason, you do not have your match by the end of say, one month from now, I will return your money."

"But this isn't a match for me, it's for my sister-in-law."

"Who is in mourning. A most difficult situation. Have you broached the subject with her?"

"Yes, but she is against it. She has no interest in being paired up with eligible men and is quite against the matter entirely."

"That will make things more difficult, though not impossible. But, Miss Harcourt, I too still wear mourning out of my love for my dearly departed husband. I would never force matchmaking on a woman who did not want it. It would be cruel."

"Then tell me how I can help her. She refuses all company aside from the family and me, or people who come to our shop. She flat out refuses to be introduced to men, and... I don't know what I can do to make her happy again."

"Perhaps she does not want to be, yet. Grieving takes time."

"I know, it's just... I don't know what to do."

"Maybe you need to allow her time to grieve. Only she can decide when it's time to accept it. You shouldn't push her to do things she's not ready to do."

Emmeline looked down at her teacup that steamed with black tea. "I know. I got my hopes up when we attended your dinner. She enjoyed the company, I think. She only minded when a gentleman wished to be introduced to her. I think it felt too forced."

Mrs. Dove-Lyon nodded. "It's possible. Has she gone often back into society since her husband died?"

"Very little. Only recently did she find the papers about the shop Anthony had purchased and signed a lease for. It was the last thing he did, so she jumped at it as a way of honoring his wishes. If she's dealing with a customer, that's fine."

"Why *else* did you want to see me?" Mrs. Dove-Lyon asked.

"I feel like she *needs* to find a way to deal with her grief. It's been five years. She only knew my brother for a year before they were married, and they only met a few times during their courtship. I have no doubt that their love and affection were genuine, but…"

"Do you feel wrong, somehow, that she is mourning your dead brother longer than you have? Is it that you believe you should continue to grieve him too, in order to match her, or measure up to her standards? Like if you did not grieve along with her, it will show the world you did not love him enough?"

Such pointed questions, Emmeline thought. "Maybe. I loved him. We had our differences, but we still cared for one another." She thought of Bedfordshire, and how her family had pulled her out of a nasty situation, sending her to London to live with Anthony and his new wife, together under one roof.

"Perhaps it is not her that needs saving, but yourself, Miss Harcourt," Mrs. Dove-Lyon said gently.

"I don't need saving. I'm fine."

A slow smile drifted across Mrs. Dove-Lyon's face. "How funny. Did I, or did I not, see you and Mr. Whittaker trading quips the other night?"

"That's one way to put it. He finds my company intolerable," Emmeline said.

"I wonder. What would you say to being matched?" Mrs. Dove-Lyon asked.

"What? With whom?"

"Anyone. Ladies pay me to find them not just any gentleman, but the right gentleman. I do not toy with people's hearts. The men and women enter into my matchmaking with their eyes open," Mrs. Dove-Lyon said.

"But why me?"

"I suspect that if your sister-in-law were to see you courting and wedded, she would be happy for you. Do you not want to be happy?"

"Of course I do, but I already am. I'm very happy with my current situation," Emmeline said.

"Is that so?"

"I don't need to be married or be courting in order to be happy."

"Quite right, you don't. But I suspect you could use some distraction in your life. You have been looking after your sister-in-law and… we could all use a bit of harmless pleasure from time to time. I tell you what. Come along to my establishment and play a few games, entertain yourself. Bring your sister-in-law along. She doesn't need to speak to anyone, and I will make it subtly known she is there for you, not to meet gentlemen. Perhaps you both might enjoy yourselves."

"With no attempt at matchmaking?" Emmeline asked.

"Not unless you ask for it."

"Thank you. I like that idea. Perhaps you're right."

"I will see you tonight, then," Mrs. Dove-Lyon said.

That afternoon, Emmeline enquired about the offices of Logan Bryant, and found his office open. She went in and was led to his large room at the back, where the door was ajar, and his loud voice could be clearly heard.

"What is the meaning of this?"

"I do not know, sir," the servant said.

"Another blasted note. Who sent it?" Mr. Bryant asked.

"Couldn't say, sir. It appeared on the doorstep."

A rustle of paper. "First it was that damn bird on the doorstep and now this. This is the third blasted letter I've had in a fortnight. What's next, blood on the door? Someone is obviously trying to get under my skin with these damned little tricks, but I'm too strong to let it bother me." He snorted. "Get out."

The door opened fully to reveal a harried servant, and Emmeline jumped as she almost collided with the man. He swept past her and as she stood in the doorway, Mr. Bryant's eyes fell on her. "What do you want?"

She came inside. "We got off on the wrong foot. I wanted to properly say hello."

He was a big man, she realized. As he sat back in his chair, his paunch threatened to burst the buttons of his russet waistcoat around his middle. His cravat was stained, and his white shirt was littered with crumbs, as was his work desk. In his hands, he held a small note and crushed it into a ball. He tossed it across the room. "Well? Go on."

"I'm Emmeline Harcourt. My late brother, Anthony, leased a shop from you on this street."

"What of it? Behind on your rent already?"

"No, nothing like that. I just wanted to say hello and welcome you to visit again."

"Hah! You really are new. No one on this street welcomes the sight of me," he said. "Do you know why?"

She shook her head.

"Because they fear me. They all tremble in their boots when I arrive. It's because I hold the keys to the kingdom. This is my street, and they all know if they put a foot wrong and produce shoddy work, or are late with their rent, I'll kick 'em out. It doesn't matter to me if they've opened a week or ten years ago. I can always find another shopkeeper to take their place."

There was no sense reasoning with him, she realized. "I see. I'm sorry, I overheard, but has a servant been threatening you?"

"No, a servant wouldn't dare. Just a nasty letter, warning me. It's useless, of course."

"Who do you think sent it?"

He shrugged. "Doesn't matter. These shopkeepers are all the same. Whiny one minute, and scraping and bowing at your boots the next. But this is the third in a month. If I find out who is behind this, I'll take them to court for harassment. No one dares harass me, and they need to learn a lesson if they think I'll forgive such behavior."

He reached into his pocket, unwrapped a lozenge, and said, "My wife recommends these. Arsenic lozenges. Takes them for her complexion and says they're good for my health. You look like you could use one. Lozenge?" He offered her one.

"No, thank you. I was wondering if maybe I could help. When did the first letter arrive?"

"Weren't you paying attention? Earlier this month. But there's no point in you helping me." He grinned. "If I want help, I'll hire a guard. Unless, that is, you want *my* help in something." He looked her up and down and licked his lips. "I'm always happy to come to a little understanding. The women find me generous, if I do say so myself."

She backed up to the door. "No, thank you. Good day." She turned and ran, his mocking laughter ringing in her ears.

THAT NIGHT, THE women dined early and dressed for going out. Emmeline wore her hair up in a pinned-back style with a pearl comb her brother had given her for Christmas one year, in a baby pink dress with a scoop bodice. She wore light pink shoes and a blush pink cloak, along with a necklace with a single pearl around her neck.

Charlotte wore her ordinary black and mauve gauzy dress, which accentuated her pale skin and long neck, and looked very fetching. She wore black shoes, black gloves, and no make-up, and the effect was almost ghostly and pale. Even if she wore a burlap sack, Emmeline realized, Charlotte would have no want of admirers that evening.

They took a carriage to Cleveland Row and got out, paying the entry fee. Allowed through the ladies' entrance, they shed their cloaks and spent a good part of the evening in the upstairs dining and gambling rooms for female guests, playing cards and drinking.

Raucous laughter could sometimes be heard from downstairs, but it soon faded amidst the chatter and gossip of their companions.

Charlotte and Emmeline spent an hour or so upstairs, then Emmeline rose, wanting to stretch her legs. She left the gambling tables and walked to the observation gallery, which offered ladies a chance to look down on the gambling floor below and feel rather special. Men and women gambled and talked, wine was shared, there was even a violinist and harpist playing spirited music while a few couples danced.

She went down to join the festivities, and accepted a glass of wine as she tried her hand at cards. She was introduced to a few gentlemen who were curious about the new face amongst them, and she smiled at one or two, but was not overly impressed by what she saw. The men were polite enough, and a few were handsome, but her heart wasn't in it.

"You look as if this entire evening has been one tedious affair," a voice said next to her.

She turned around. "Mr. Whittaker." She curtsied.

He bowed. "What brings you back to the Lyon's Den? Hoping to meet your true love?"

"What if I were?"

"Don't let me stop you. Although I doubt you will find that here."

"What makes you say that?" she asked.

"These are men of quality. They will want more than a pretty face to attract them."

"Are you saying that I'm pretty, or not pretty enough?" She glared at him.

"Your feminine charms are offset by your obstinate nature," he told her. "Are you really hoping to meet your match here? Did you pay Mrs. Dove-Lyon for the pleasure?"

"No, not exactly. She invited my sister-in-law and me to dine and amuse ourselves."

He grabbed her arm and whirled her toward him.

"What are you doing?" she demanded, when she heard a commotion behind her and a cry. She turned around to see a servant had slipped and narrowly missed spilling a drink on her. By pulling her away, Mr. Whittaker had done her a favor.

He held her arm tightly, keeping her out of harm's way. "Be careful where you're walking," he told the servant, who quickly picked up the fallen glass and scurried away, as another came to clean the mess.

She glanced at him, taking in the sight of his curled, light brown hair, almost reddish in the golden candlelight. The gleam of his white cravat, finely tied at his throat, and the deep red of his waistcoat, almost crimson in the light. His face was cleanshaven, but somehow, she found it too trying, and rather wished he'd kept some of the fuzz on his chin from the day before.

She looked down where he gripped her arm. "Thank you. You can release me now."

"What? Oh." He let go of her arm as if she were an annoying fly. "Try to pay attention. I would not add clumsiness to your list of charms for suitors."

She blushed. "I was not clumsy, I—"

"That's it, which one of you did it? Who stole it?" A loud, familiar voice could be heard over the din.

"What's going on?" Emmeline asked.

"I don't know," Mr. Whittaker said. "Stay here."

He walked toward the sound and frowned as Emmeline followed. "I told you to stay put."

"You are not my brother or my father."

His mouth set in a firm line. "Do you always disobey?"

"When it's in my interest."

They frowned at each other, and both walked toward the noise. At the center of the commotion stood Mr. Bryant, who said loudly, "Where is it? Which one of you took it?"

Mrs. Dove-Lyon appeared, along with a number of servants.

"What is the matter?"

Logan stood and stabbed a finger in the air. "The matter is that someone has stolen something precious from me. My wife's comb has been stolen. Somebody here took it." His gaze fell on Mr. Whittaker and Emmeline. "And I know who."

CHAPTER THREE

EMMELINE AND MR. Whittaker looked at Mr. Bryant, who stood red-faced, his hands clenched at his sides. He pointed at Mr. Whittaker. "This man did it. Mrs. Dove-Lyon, arrest this man."

Heads turned to look at Mr. Whittaker. "Me? What did I steal?"

"My wife's comb." Mr. Bryant marched up to him. "I know it was you. Don't try to deny it."

But Mr. Whittaker had no time for him. He stared at something in the distance and staggered.

Emmeline took his arm, catching him. "Mr. Whittaker, are you all right?"

"I'm fine," he grunted, and leaned against her, holding onto her arm. "Too much wine is all."

But the blood had drained from his face, he looked so pale. It was not the wine, Emmeline could tell.

Instead, his gaze fell to the woman standing behind Mr. Bryant. "Lucinda."

A woman with luscious reddish-brown hair coiled at the nape of her neck, wearing a rich dress that bordered on red, so deep was its color. Her square bodice was trimmed with black lace, but it was clear this was for effect, not an indication of mourning. Her skirt's hem and sleeves were equally trimmed, and she wore a shawl with gold embroidered thread that caught the light and carried a fan. At the sight of Mr. Whittaker, she dropped the fan to the floor. "Horatio."

Emmeline glanced at Mr. Whittaker, but he had no time for her. Instead, he strode past Mr. Bryant and picked up her fan, handing it to Mrs. Bryant.

"Thank you." Her gloved hands touched his as she accepted the fan, her eyes barely leaving his face.

He grunted and stepped back. "What were you saying?"

Mr. Bryant's eyes narrowed. "This man has taken something valuable from me. Tell him, Lucinda."

Her eyes never leaving Mr. Whittaker, the woman said, "My comb is missing. It's a comb with a ruby in it. It's very valuable." She shrugged her shawl up higher on her shoulders, drawing attention to her pale skin that practically glowed in the candlelight.

"I'm sure there has just been a simple misunderstanding. My guests would never steal." Mrs. Dove-Lyon said. "They know better than to sully my house with such low behavior."

"Are you so sure? I wish I had your confidence, Mrs. Dove-Lyon, but alas, I know this young man. And unfortunately, I know him to have less than honorable intentions. I demand you search him," Mr. Bryant said.

Mrs. Bryant put a hand on her husband's arm. "Logan, don't," but she was shaken off.

"Search me? What are you playing at, Bryant? I never touched her. I certainly didn't steal it," Mr. Whittaker said.

"Then turn out your pockets and prove it. Or else I shall call the watch," Mr. Bryant said.

Mr. Whittaker turned out his pockets. "See? No comb."

Mr. Bryant's face turned red. He jabbed a finger at Mrs. Dove-Lyon. "I demand you find my wife's comb immediately. Or I shall tell everyone that you allow thieves into your den. See how many patrons you have after that."

Mrs. Dove-Lyon's face could have been carved from stone. "I do not take kindly to threats, sir. Nor do I appreciate your accusing my guests of theft without proof."

"My wife's comb is missing. What else could it have been?" Mr. Bryant asked.

People in the room looked around and muttered amongst themselves. A low murmur circulated around the room, and even the music stopped playing.

"I can help," Emmeline said loudly.

"You? What can you do? You're just a silly girl." Mr. Bryant looked down his nose at her.

Emmeline frowned. "We lose things in our shop all the time. I bet I could find what you're looking for."

Mr. Bryant snorted, while Mr. Whittaker glanced at her. Mrs. Dove-Lyon said, "That is very good of you, Miss Harcourt."

Mrs. Dove-Lyon took her aside and said quietly, "Do you really think you can find it? I cannot abide rudeness in my den, and I will not tolerate theft."

"Mr. Whittaker is innocent. He was standing with me and didn't even notice Mrs. Bryant until after the theft was announced."

"I agree. I'd like both of you to work together to find out who stole it, if it is missing."

"What do you mean?"

"This is not the first time Mr. Bryant has caused trouble, although it is the first time he has accused one of my guests of stealing. I wonder if he has created a fuss just because he likes a bit of drama in his life."

Emmeline raised an eyebrow. "Mr. Whittaker?"

"I'll do whatever it takes to clear my name. And prove that man wrong," he muttered.

"Excellent. I was standing near them when the event happened and clearly recall seeing Mrs. Bryant's ruby comb. I thought it was rather pretty, it caught the light so. I, of course, would never steal, so I believe we can discount myself and Mr. Whittaker as suspects. The only people who were nearby who could have taken it are Mr. Forrest, Miss Lott, Mr. Ponsonby, and Mrs. Jonas. Oh and Mr. Bryant, I suppose."

"We'll find out who did this," Emmeline said.

"Please hurry. I cannot risk rumors of theft to be associated with my institution. I would consider it a personal favor if you did this." Mrs. Dove-Lyon nodded and left, speaking with two servants.

"Well, that's a pretty mess you've landed us in. Mind telling me why you've dragged me into this too?" Mr. Whittaker asked.

"I didn't. Mrs. Dove-Lyon suggested it. Besides, you're innocent. Don't you want to help me puzzle this out?" Emmeline asked, "Unless, of course, you've got something better to do."

He grunted and scratched his face. "Let's do this. Where first?"

"Let's speak with Mr. Forrest."

The man in question was a young man with round spectacles, who habitually pushed them up his nose. "Oh, hello."

"Nasty business this," Mr. Whittaker said.

"Oh, yes. Terrible. But the young lady didn't help herself much. If you ask me, she was asking for trouble."

"What do you mean?" Emmeline asked.

"Well, if you don't mind my saying so, she received so many compliments on the comb, she was often taking it out of her hair and showing it around to people, so they could admire the ruby in the light. I admired it too, but..." he looked away. "I didn't need to for long," Mr. Forrest whispered. "It's fake."

"Fake?" Emmeline said. Then she whispered, "What do you mean?"

"I make a study of rocks and gemstones. What the earth has to tell us is wondrous, and um, I work at a jeweler's in town. Anyway, I make it my business to value stones, especially if a man is buying a quality piece for the lady in his life, or if a person wishes to sell." He swallowed and said, "That ruby is fake. Very flashy and pretty, but it's an ordinary rock."

"I see. Thank you." Emmeline turned and approached Miss Lott. Emmeline recognized her as the pretty redhead who had talked to Mr. Whittaker at dinner before. For some irrational reason, she disliked her but could not say why.

Mr. Whittaker looked less happy to see her. "Hello, Miss Lott."

"Oh, hello, Mr. Whittaker. What a funny thing. Here we are, thrown together again." she giggled. "Almost like it was fate."

Mr. Whittaker winced and looked away.

"Did you see what happened with the comb, Miss Lott?"

"Oh, no. I mean yes. I mean…" She tapped her chin with a slim finger. "Well, she was showing it around an awful lot. I didn't see who took, it, but it did look rather pretty."

"You wouldn't have wanted it for yourself?" Mr. Whittaker asked.

"Me? Oh, I suppose so. But I wouldn't dare take something that didn't belong to me. And besides, Mrs. Bryant is ever so nice. She offered to let me wear it in my hair to see how it catches the light, but I wouldn't let her give it to me. I told her, no, thank you."

"Why?"

"Um. I'm a trifle forgetful at times. I wouldn't want to be accused of stealing when I'd have just forgotten to take it out and return it to her. And now, of course, it has happened, and you're asking questions trying to find out who did it. Am I right?"

"Yes."

"I knew it. I thought you had a studious eye." She patted her hair, which was pinned up in an elaborate style. "Say, you don't mind checking my hair, do you? To see if it's there by mistake?"

"Not at all. Allow me." Mr. Whittaker glanced over. "No. No ruby comb."

36

"Oh, that's a relief. I mean not for your search, but it is for me. Jolly good. Well, good luck." She smiled prettily at Mr. Whittaker and walked off in search of the nearest drink.

Emmeline smiled at Mr. Whittaker. "You have an admirer."

"Don't remind me."

"She did have very pretty hair."

He glowered at her. "Come along." He walked to Mr. Ponsonby, a fellow who unfortunately resembled an egg, with a round bottom, a stomach that hung over his blue trousers, round red cheeks, and tufts of blond hair. He stood by a buffet, filling his plate with pastries and cakes.

At the mention of his name, he turned, shedding crumbs. His plate was stacked with a rather impressive tower of pastries, and his mouth was full as he glanced at them both with a limpid expression. "Yes?"

"We wondered if you knew anything about Mrs. Bryant's missing ruby comb," Emmeline started.

"No. I thought it was a pretty piece of jewelry, but when I saw she wasn't selling, I lost interest. She made it sound as though she had a piece she wanted to sell, and I always pride myself on amassing the finest quality items. She had hinted she wanted to sell, but when her husband insisted she just show off her comb, I left her to it."

Mr. Whittaker thanked him and turned to leave, when Emmeline asked, "Was she often in the habit of selling her jewelry?"

Mr. Ponsonby's eyes darted to Mrs. Bryant over her shoulder, and he gave a full shake of his head and said loudly, "No, of course not. To even suggest such a thing is laughable." He gave a little laugh, then muttered, "She has occasionally tired of the odd piece of jewelry here and there. I simply offered her a fair price."

"I see. Would you have wanted the ruby comb if she had offered it?"

He shrugged. "Perhaps. But I'm not hard up, if that's what you're wondering. I didn't steal it. I don't need to steal to get my wares. The owners find me." He popped a piece of pastry into his mouth.

"Who do you think stole it?"

"If I had to guess, Miss Lott would be my choice. She seems too eager and likes pretty things. It wouldn't surprise me if she had sticky fingers. But then, there is also Mrs. Jonas who was nearby, and everyone knows she is an outrageous gossip. She might have seen something."

To Mrs. Jonas they went. She was an older woman, with short brown hair fading to gray, her face lined but still pretty, with an expression of knowing something the others didn't. She took a sip of a glass of wine and smirked. "I wondered when you two would come to me."

Mr. Whittaker gave her a charming smile. "We should have asked you from the start. What do you know about this matter of the ruby comb?"

The older woman smiled, the red wine staining her mouth. "I saw everything. From Mrs. Bryant's little nod to Mr. Ponsonby, to her showing off the comb to Miss Lott and Mr. Forrest, and then Mr. Bryant's taking it back. He was so forceful. It was a wonder the little comb didn't snap in his hands when he took it."

"And then?"

"There was a lot of discussion. She reached for it. The comb could have changed hands. I didn't see it at that point, as Mr. Bryant had already raised the cry of it being stolen." She looked at him. "What I want to know is, what does he have against you, Mr. Whittaker? You were across the room. There's no way you could have taken the comb, so why did he point the finger at you? That's what *I* want to know."

Mr. Whittaker tensed and took a step back. "There is nothing between us, Mrs. Jonas. Nothing at all."

"I know a story when I hear one. Come now, you can tell me. What is it?"

"Nothing to concern you, Mrs. Jonas," Mr. Whittaker said, an annoyed tilt to his chin. His very manner was stiff and formal. "Excuse me."

"Well, I never," Mrs. Jonas remarked as Mr. Whittaker turned on his heel, and left them standing there. "You will tell me if you learn what it is that is bothering him. There's a story there, I can tell."

Emmeline mumbled a response, she wasn't sure what, and followed Mr. Whittaker back into the crowd of people.

Mrs. Dove-Lyon approached them. "Have you figured out who did it?"

"I think so. There's just one person we have left to talk to." Emmeline looked at Mr. Bryant, who strode toward them.

"Well? Have you found who took my wife's comb?"

"Logan, please. There's no need for this. I—" Mrs. Bryant started.

He cut her off. "One of these people took your comb. I will know who, or I will call the nearest constable to take them all in for questioning. I'll have you know that Magistrate Tomlinson is a close personal friend," he declared loudly.

Emmeline surveyed him and felt Mr. Whittaker's presence beside her. He was quiet and steady, but she knew he was ready for a fight if need be. It was comforting, somehow. Knowing he was there, even if they were usually at odds. Strange, it was almost like she could trust him.

"Mr. Bryant, I wonder. Did you happen to see who took the comb?" Emmeline asked. Beside her, she was conscious of Mr. Whittaker holding his breath, as if frozen before a snake.

"No, of course I didn't. Why else would I demand the thief be caught? Honestly, this is absurd. I don't know what sort of establishment you're running here—" he said to Mrs. Dove-Lyon.

"You see, the reason I ask is because we have spoken to all the possible people who could have done it, and yet it seems as though one person was left holding the comb."

"Who?" Mr. Forrest asked.

"Yes, who? Tell us," Mr. Bryant said.

"You, Mr. Bryant. You saw your wife remove the comb and allow others to admire it in the light, like Miss Lott hoping to wear it, Mr. Forrest to admire the gemstone, and even Mr. Ponsonby to consider its value, should she ever tire of it."

His face pulled into an angry snarl.

"But when you realized she had attracted the wrong sort of admirers, each with a different motive, you knew you had to put a stop to it. So you raised a fuss and declared it stolen," Emmeline said.

"Don't be ridiculous. Why would I declare the damn thing stolen if it wasn't?"

"Precisely what I want to know. Would you turn out your pockets, please?" she asked.

Mr. Bryant stared at her in surprise. "Me? You dare ask me that?"

"I do, sir. If you wouldn't mind."

He balked and looked at Mr. Whittaker, Mrs. Dove-Lyon, and the number of burly and athletic card dealers and servants who stood by, watching. He shoved his hands in his pockets, and he stiffened. He paused as his face turned red.

"Oh, let me." Mrs. Bryant pulled out his hand to see and revealed the comb.

"It's there!" Mrs. Jonas said, pointing. "He had it the whole time."

"What sorry trick is this?" Mr. Forrest asked.

"It's no trick. I thought for sure it had been stolen. All of you were swarming around her like vultures. Is it any wonder I thought it was one of you?" Mr. Bryant said.

"I tried to tell you, Logan, but you wouldn't listen. I thought it ended up in your pocket."

"Why didn't you say anything?" He turned on her.

"You refused to pay attention when I tried talking to you. It's like talking to a brick wall sometimes," Lucinda said.

He gritted his teeth, his posture stiff as he held out the comb. She snatched it and tucked it back in her hair.

"If you knew where it was this whole time, why let us go around questioning people?" Emmeline asked.

Lucinda shrugged. "Perhaps I wanted to see how you'd do. A woman going around asking questions is a bit of an oddity. I suppose you're not as dumb as you look." She gave Mr. Whittaker a shy smile.

He said, "You should have spoken up."

"And Mr. Whittaker deserves an apology," Emmeline said, looking at Mr. Bryant, who laughed.

"If you think I'm apologizing to him, you've got a long wait." He smirked.

"Well I, for one, am glad this was resolved. Thank you, Mr. Whittaker and Miss Harcourt, for your fast deductions. It was most enlightening," Mrs. Dove-Lyon said. "Mr. Bryant, if I might have a word."

She led him away from the others, but not before he said, "I know one of you is behind these little tricks. This was just a test to see which of you was guilty. I know." He tapped his nose and followed Mrs. Dove-Lyon.

Lucinda exhaled loudly and helped herself to a glass of wine. She drank, then exhaled loudly. "Well, you can be sure I'll be hearing about that for the next few days. It really was impressive, Horatio," she said, looking up at him.

Emmeline's eyebrows rose at the sight of the married woman, closing the distance between them.

Mr. Whittaker, for his part, looked supremely uncomfortable. He stepped back and coughed. "Forgive me, Mrs. Bryant, but it was all Miss Harcourt's doing."

"Who?"

"Miss Harcourt. We are courting." Mr. Whittaker took Emmeline's hand in his and pressed it to his lips.

CHAPTER FOUR

"WHAT?" MISS HARCOURT sputtered at the same time as Mrs. Bryant said, "You? You are courting?" She stared at their joined hands as if they had offered her a snake.

"Yes," Mr. Whittaker said stiffly, "we are."

Emmeline swallowed. "I—"

"We did not want to say anything, especially considering your comb having gone missing," he said.

Mrs. Bryant's smile was sweet. "How very kind. Congratulations." Hurt flashed across her face and she whirled and walked away.

Emmeline waited until Mrs. Bryant was out of earshot before she whispered to Mr. Whittaker. "Courting? Are you mad?"

"No. It seemed like the best possible solution." He released her hand.

"You are out of your senses. You don't know me. You don't even like me. I don't like you," she said.

The right corner of his mouth curled into a half-smile. "You could grow to like me."

She stared at him. "You clearly have drunk too much wine. You're being ridiculous."

"Not at all." He took her arm and led her to one of the empty gambling tables, and procured them glasses of wine. To the average observer, it would appear as though they were simply chatting. No one would know any different.

His gray-blue eyes sought hers. "I have a proposition for you."

She rolled her eyes. "I need more wine for this." She drank, swallowed too fast, and coughed, setting her glass down on the table.

He handed her a small handkerchief, and she accepted it, using it to dab at her mouth and cough into. Once her small fit stopped, her eyes were streaming, and her face felt hot.

"Are you all right?" he asked.

"I'm fine." She offered him the handkerchief, but he shook his head.

"Keep it."

"Very well." She folded it. "You were saying?"

"We should court."

She dropped the handkerchief to the floor. He picked it up and handed it to her, and she tucked it into her reticule that hung from her wrist. "I didn't hear you right. I thought you said..."

He repeated himself.

"Why on earth would you suggest such a thing?" she asked.

A grin warred with seriousness on his face. "I should have thought of this before. We both have something the other can help with."

She stepped back, bumping into the gambling table. "I don't know what you're thinking, but I am not that sort of girl."

He shook his head. "You don't understand." He looked around. Once satisfied there were no people nearby, he said, "We could help each other."

"How would us courting achieve anything?" she asked.

"The more you come here, the more people will think you are after a marriage proposal. Congratulations, you'll soon earn one. Have you thought about what you will do when that happens?"

She blinked at him.

"That's what I thought. You wouldn't know the first thing about how to respond," he said.

"With an attitude like that, I can't understand why the women aren't falling after you in droves," she said.

His eyebrows furrowed. "I've done it. I've been rude again, haven't I?"

"A bit. But you're not alone. Why would you want to court me?"

"Perhaps you are not so unlikeable as you think... Besides, we would just pretend."

"What for?"

He ran a hand through his tousled brown hair.

"Does this have something to do with that woman, Mrs. Bryant?" she asked.

He looked at her and let out a breath. "Somewhat. We are acquainted, let's leave it at that. But Miss Harcourt, you are willfully obtuse, and I am... never mind. It would serve me well to have others, like Mrs. Bryant, see that I am happily courting a pretty young woman. I believe we can help one another. If we just pretend for a bit, then we can avoid any misunderstandings or attention from other people we do not want."

That did hold a certain appeal. She blushed as she realized he'd called her pretty.

"Well?" he asked.

"I'm thinking about it." She gave him a sidelong glance. "Why me?"

"I beg your pardon?"

"There are many fine, pretty young women here. Miss Lott would accept you in a second. Why me, when we can barely get along for five minutes without disagreeing?"

"Maybe I like a bit of disagreement," he grumbled.

"Maybe you're not telling me the whole story."

He bowed his head in acquiescence. "There is some truth to that. I might tell you the story when the time is right. Could you consider this to be a favor to me, for now?"

"What do I get out of it?"

"So mercenary," he commented, eyeing her. "I should think that would be obvious."

She waited.

He leaned against the gambling table and gave her a winning smile. "I am not without my attractions."

She laughed. "Pray, do tell." It amused her to see a flash of discomfort cross his face. Such arrogance deserved to be poked and prodded at.

She looked him up and down, openly. Brazenly, even. She suspected that to do so would annoy him, and for some reason, she wished to rile him. She slowly took in the sight of his polished black boots, his smart gray trousers and creamy-colored waistcoat, with a slate-gray suit jacket to match. A prim white cravat hung at his neck, and his fair skin was marred by a single pockmark near the left of his nose.

Otherwise, his slight nose, his firm chin, his expertly trimmed sideburns with a bit of fuzz on the chin, and the way his tousled hair sat arranged, it all spoke of a care for his appearance without excessive vanity. He had a care for how he looked, but not too much. She could appreciate that.

She could appreciate even more the way his broad shoulders filled out his suit jacket, and how he leaned against the table with the grace of an athletic man, but with a wolfish smile. The sense she had was of a bear or wild animal trapped in a man's clothing. If he were proposing something, she would need all her wits to match him. To her surprise, she was already enjoying the idea of it.

"You mean physically?" she asked.

"That, and my reputation. I... can afford to entertain you in style.

You will not be disappointed if we were to begin courting."

He was alluding to his wealth, she realized. What an ego.

"Why not choose Miss Lott, or one of the other women here? As you say, you have your attractions," she said with a smile.

He glanced over at the assembled guests and a slight frown crossed his face. "I do not think I could tolerate one of those empty-headed women for long. They are indeed pretty to look at, but with little conversation aside from the style of their dress, the number of couples dancing, or the state of the weather. I think I would go mad."

She raised an eyebrow.

"You at least, I can hold a conversation with. However disagreeable."

"High praise indeed." She snorted. "At least you are honest."

"Surely this plan would hold some appeal for you as well. Can you truly say you would not be better off in the short term being associated with me?" he asked confidently. "Or is it that you have never been asked before, and are overcome?"

She cocked her head at him, feeling a warmth to her cheeks. "You have a high opinion of yourself."

He laughed, a curt sound. "I have reason to." He looked at her. "I don't offer this lightly, and I may change my mind. So what do you say? Do you accept?" He held out his hand.

She looked at him. A beat passed, then two. A flicker of disappointment crossed his face. He dropped his hand, turned, and began to walk away, when she said, "Wait."

He turned back around.

"If I do this, I would like your help," she said.

"In what?"

"Choosing a good person," she told him.

"For your sister?" he asked.

"For me."

Now it was his eyebrows which rose. "You don't think you are choosing well, now?"

She pursed her lips. She found him utterly disagreeable, and couldn't imagine being with a man like him. He was persistently annoying and arrogant in everything.

"I mean it, for real. Not a fake courtship. What you are proposing is little more than a business agreement between partners. If I help you, then I'd like you to help me back. In return."

"You want to get married?" he asked.

"I want you to help me find a good person to enter a relationship with. I have made mistakes in the past." She looked away.

"I see. Very well. Let's shake on it." He held out a hand.

She took it. He raised her fingers to his lips. She tensed, and he released her hand.

"What was that? That wasn't a handshake," she said.

He gave her a wolfish grin again. "We are courting now. I will help you find a person of good character to throw me over for, but I mean to enjoy myself in the meantime."

Her eyes widened and she snatched her hand back, rubbing it on her thigh. "Don't make me regret this," she warned.

"You won't. You'll be having too much fun," he quipped.

Word of their courtship traveled fast, and in no time at all, people came up to congratulate them. Emmeline smiled demurely and made the acquaintance of many young men and envious women, as she was introduced as the girl being courted by Mr. Whittaker. It seemed that Mr. Whittaker was well connected with the guests of the Lyon's Den.

She could hear the music playing and tapped her foot along, and sensed Mr. Whittaker's eyes on her. She looked at him, but he said stiffly, "I do not dance."

"Why not?" she asked.

He frowned and said nothing, when a sweet voice said behind them, "Because, Mr. Whittaker never dances. He has never danced a day in his life, isn't that right, Whittaker?"

Emmeline looked to find Mrs. Bryant behind them, leaning against a gambling table.

"That is absurd," Mr. Whittaker said, glancing back at her.

"My mistake. Perhaps it is that you've never found a dance partner worthy of your attention," Mrs. Bryant teased.

Mr. Whittaker's face reddened, and he stood stiffly, staring straight ahead.

"But then, you would know that, since you are courting," Mrs. Bryant said sweetly.

Mr. Bryant approached and smirked. "Lucinda, stop teasing poor Mr. Whittaker. You'll make him blush. I do not think anyone could tempt Mr. Whittaker to dance."

Emmeline sensed rather than saw Mr. Whittaker's hands clench. She said, "Well, I love to dance, but I do not feel like it this evening. In fact, I'd like some fresh air. Mr. Whittaker, could you show me the balcony? I should like to admire the view of London."

"It would be my pleasure." He held out an arm and they walked together, eyes straight ahead, ignoring the watchful looks of Mr. and Mrs. Bryant.

She matched her pace to his, allowing the folds of her long gown to swish around her legs as she walked, so it was a pretty sight. She kept her head high and lightly rested her hand in the crook of his elbow. It felt rock hard, and she wanted to glance over and ask if he was all right, but she didn't dare. His face could have been carved from stone.

He led her across the main gambling room and out to a wide set of glass doors that led out to a private balcony. As he opened the doors, a refreshing breath of chilly night air gave a shock to her senses, and she released him from her touch, moving forward to grasp the narrow, black-swirled railings.

They did not speak for a time, simply breathing in the sights of the London night. Eventually he let out a noisy breath in the cool air and leaned forward, resting his hands against the sturdy railing. "Thank you."

"They like to tease you," she said.

"They like to see me as the butt of a joke. I am their chosen fool," he said disgustedly.

"Why do you tolerate their japes? Why do you not respond back? I know you have the temper for it."

He looked at her, and she smiled.

"I…" he paused.

"Will you not tell me what that was about?"

"No. Let us just say that I do not care to dance, and that is all there is to it." He crossed his arms over his chest.

She glanced back through the windows. To her surprise, she saw Charlotte standing on the sidelines, talking with a young man.

"Who is that?" Emmeline asked.

"Who?"

"That young man, standing with my sister-in-law."

"That? Matthew Nevitt. Why?" he asked.

"What does he mean by talking to her? She's in mourning."

"I imagine he is enjoying her pretty face and conversation," Mr. Whittaker said.

It was true. Either her sister-in-law had come down to look for her and gotten waylaid, or she had somehow met the young man by chance. Either way, he looked particularly interested in her, but Emmeline disliked him immediately.

She spied him wearing a ridiculous suit of forest green, with a tangerine-colored waistcoat and shining buttons that caught the light. He rather stunned her eyes with his garish attire. He wore white silk knee socks that showed a thin calf which bespoke a runner's gait, and he had a pointed chin. He wore his light brown hair back in a loose queue with some carefully selected strands framing his face. The effect was comely indeed, and far too staged.

She imagined he must have practiced his look in the mirror, and ordered his valet to arrange his hair just so. She disliked the very sight of him.

"What do you know about him?"

"Mr. Nevitt? A good shot. Likes to hunt."

She glanced at him.

He shrugged. "He likes a good game, especially when there's a prize to be had. The harder the quarry, the more he likes it."

"Does he always get what he wants?"

"You mean, does he ever lose? It's rare. Why?"

"I want him to stay away from my sister-in-law."

He smiled. "From the looks of it, she doesn't mind the attention."

It was true. She did seem to be enjoying herself and was laughing at something he said.

They re-entered the room. Mr. Whittaker promised to call on her the next day, and together she and Charlotte collected their cloaks and waited outside the front steps of the ladies' entrance for a hackney carriage.

Emmeline saw Mr. Bryant walk out as well from a different exit, and the flickering light as he lit up a pipe. The subtle hint of tobacco scented the air. A carriage turned the corner, the sound of horses' hooves clattering against the cobblestone streets. Emmeline watched as, all of a sudden, a small and curvy dark figure lurched at Mr. Bryant like a fiend on a stage, sending him straight into the path of the carriage.

He stumbled and fell, landing on his hands and knees. He got up, looked, and threw himself out of the way just as the carriage pulled to a screeching stop, the horses neighing at the sharp tug of their reins against their harnesses.

Emmeline was at his side in an instant. "Mr. Bryant."

He looked at her, his expression wild with fear. The lantern's light played dark shadows against his features, and she helped him to his feet, never minding the dirt and grime that transferred to her gloves and cloak from his damp hands.

"Are you all right?" she asked.

He huffed and coughed, pulling his loose cravat looser. His coat and waistcoat were open, the buttons having come loose and flying during his fall. "Did you see what happened? That carriage driver's mad. He could have killed me."

She stood by as he coughed and brushed dirt and muck from his clothes. Mud and the remnants of horse dung and hay stuck to his trousers, making Emmeline wrinkle her nose.

Mrs. Bryant flew to his side. "Darling, what happened to you?"

"Never mind," he muttered, and shook his fist at the carriage driver.

Once the driver had ascertained he was still alive, he shrugged and asked if they wanted a hackney.

"As if I'd accept a ride from you when you almost ran me over. Watch where you're looking next time," Mr. Bryant growled.

The carriage driver uttered a sharp reply.

Charlotte came to stand by Emmeline. "Is that our carriage?"

Realizing he was at risk of losing a ride, Mr. Bryant said roughly, "No, it's mine." He threw the carriage doors open and climbed in, tugging his wife after him. The carriage door snapped shut, and a loud banging on the roof signaled the start of the journey.

The carriage took off at pace, rumbling down the cobblestones once more.

"It figures," Charlotte said beside her, shaking her head. "That man will have his own way, in everything. Even when he could have died falling into that carriage. He could have been run over. He could have…" Her voice faltered.

Emmeline took her sister-in-law's hand. "I know."

"What's wrong, Emmy? You look like something terrible has happened. Did you fall, too?"

"No, not me," Emmeline said.

"Oh, but your gloves and cloak are dirty, I see. That's nothing the servants can't handle."

"No, I'm fine."

"Then why do you look so distracted?" Charlotte asked.

"It's not me, Charlotte. It's Mr. Bryant." Emmeline paused, watching the carriage disappear into the night. "He didn't fall. He was pushed."

CHAPTER FIVE

E MMELINE WAS QUIET all the way home.

She rather preferred the darkness of night, and the quiet comfort of the carriage, feeling it bounce and jolt as the driver took them through the London streets and into Cheapside.

She looked out the window but did not remember anything she saw, and distantly heard Charlotte's discussion of the gambling wins and losses she had witnessed, or the dancing she watched, or the delightful young man she had met that evening.

Instead, thoughts of Mr. Bryant filled her mind. Who would want to hurt him, and why? He could have died. Was it an accident, or had he been pushed? Now that the event had passed, she began to question what she had seen.

She remembered the fearful expression on his face as she had helped him up from the street. His hair was messy, his eyes wild, and he'd hesitated before accepting her offer of help. That didn't stop him from taking the carriage he'd almost been run over by, but she hadn't expected any thanks from him.

Her mind was made up; he was a loud, proud man who liked to throw his weight around. He felt himself to be a man of importance, a businessman, and wanted people in the vicinity to know it. He had a pretty wife on his arm and bedecked her in jewels, but what was the reason for his teasing of Mr. Whittaker? His little remarks and smirks held amused barbs and thinly veiled animosity behind the jibes, and she wondered what had happened to create such mutual dislike between the two men.

The next day was Sunday. After attending church and taking a small luncheon with her sister-in-law, they sat in the small parlor, which Charlotte had redecorated following her husband's death five years ago. The walls now were a light shade of pink and bore small pictures of silk flowers Charlotte had painted. She'd never been one for sketches, landscapes, or portraits, but she did like miniature flowers.

There was a knock at the door. A servant announced, "A Mr. Whittaker, to see Miss Harcourt."

Charlotte looked up from her book. "Why is he here?"

Emmeline swallowed. "We are... That is..."

Mr. Whittaker entered the room. "Good day." He bowed.

The girls rose and curtsied. "What a pleasure to see you, Mr. Whittaker. I didn't expect to see you so soon."

He said nothing, and surveyed the room, taking in the small but serviceable fireplace, the elegant screen in front of it, the painted silks framed around the room, the comfortable chairs and low white sofa, and wooden table, the worn rug that covered the majority of the floor, as well as the long narrow windows that let in the sunlight. The day had been dreary that morning but had cleared up after lunch.

"There is an exhibition at the Royal Academy. I wondered if you both might like to join me."

"Oh, yes. I should like that very much. Emmy?" Charlotte asked.

Emmeline looked at her partner in deception. "I should be glad to join you, Mr. Whittaker."

Once bedecked in smart bonnets and walking cloaks, he escorted them outside and opened the carriage door. Charlotte stepped inside the carriage and took her seat. Emmeline moved toward the step, when Mr. Whittaker suddenly took her free hand and helped her up. She glanced back at him and then down at his hand, which held hers firmly. She blinked, accepted his help, and stepped inside, feeling subtly odd as he climbed in and sat across from her.

Once at the Royal Academy, Mr. Whittaker paid the entry fee for the three of them, despite Emmeline's offer to pay their own way.

"Oh, let him pay already, Emmy," Charlotte hushed her when she protested. "He's trying to be kind. When was the last time a man did something nice for you?"

Emmeline shot her sister-in-law a look. That comment felt like a loaded statement. What was she playing at? Unlike her relation, who seemed quite happy to be taken care of, Emmeline did not want to be indebted to anyone, including Mr. Whittaker. Emmeline stood by as Charlotte chatted to him as they walked from room to room.

The academy was filled with stunning sculptures and the walls were filled with dozens of fine pieces of art. Landscapes, portraits, religious tableaus, and pictures of wild animals or even fantastical beasts filled the canvases, some looking as though they might leap out of the frames at any second.

Mr. Whittaker stopped short as they were about to approach a painting. It was of a young woman, a peasant girl who didn't just stare at the viewer, she glared at them, as if they dared mock her with their eyes, interrupting her work. She held a quill and book in her hands, a thin shawl was loosely knotted and hung at her back, and her dark hair spilled out of a poorly tied blue headwrap. In the scene, it was as if the viewer had stepped into another time and disturbed the poor maid at her work, earning her ire.

Emmeline drank in the sight. Charlotte joined her, then moved on, but Mr. Whittaker stayed at her side, not speaking.

"I love this piece."

"Do you? What about it?" he asked.

"I like the way she glares at me, as if it's my fault for the mistake she's about to make. We might have disturbed her and caused her to knock over her inkwell, or made her write with too much ink in her book, and now she must blot it out. I like her face, her expression."

"I do too," he admitted.

It was a subtle twist of the lips, but if one looked closely enough at her fair skin and patient expression, a person could note the angled eyebrow, aimed downward in disgust, the annoyed tilt of her head. The artist had captured her expression well. As a subject, she did not feel like a stationary piece of art painted on canvas. It was like looking through a window, and seeing an annoyed servant look back at her.

"I've never liked that painting," a woman said behind them.

They turned. Lucinda Bryant stood there, a slight, amused turn to her lips, as if she saw something funny, but Emmeline knew not what. She wore a light brown walking cloak and smart chocolate brown hat that had a stiff horn shape, a light brown ribbon around the middle, and a tiny sprig of flowers on the side. She looked very smart, and knew it. Her brown hair curled around her shoulders becomingly, and her mouth was pursed like a rosebud, or as if she were about to lay a kiss on someone.

"What are you doing here, Mr. Whittaker?" Mrs. Bryant stood there, greedily drinking in the sight of him. "Oh. Hello, Miss Harcourt, I didn't see you there."

Too busy looking at Mr. Whittaker, she thought. "Hello, Mrs. Bryant. Is your husband well?"

"What an odd question. Of course he is. Why would you ask that?"

"After his stumble in the street yesterday evening, I thought he might be tired," Emmeline said.

Mrs. Bryant's eyes narrowed. "I shall be sure to convey your best wishes for his health." She huffed. "Horatio, a word."

Mr. Whittaker flushed and muttered, "Excuse me," then walked after Mrs. Bryant, who crooked a finger at him to follow, before striding across the room.

"Insufferable," Emmeline said, just as Charlotte said, "Oh, you've met Mrs. Bryant, I see. She seems so nice. I didn't know you knew each other."

"We met the other night at Mrs. Dove-Lyon's establishment," Emmeline said, looking around. "I'm not sure about her."

"Well, I understand you may doubt yourself, but you should make an effort, especially as she seems to be a close acquaintance of Mr. Whittaker's. I say, do you think they are merely good friends, or something more?" Charlotte asked with an impish smile.

"I couldn't say. Charlotte..." Emmeline started. "There's something I should tell you."

"Whatever it is, it can wait. Now come, I want to see the paintings over there." Charlotte motioned for her to follow and walked on.

HORATIO STOOD STIFFLY by Mrs. Bryant, the actress he'd formerly known as Lucinda Cross. She still wore the same floral perfume that had driven him mad, once upon a time. Now the scent and being near her almost gave him physical pain.

Lucinda stood nearby, looking at a painting, but like any consummate actress, he knew it was all a guise. A pretty picture for any onlooker who happened to pass by. She knew exactly how to stand and pose, how to angle her gloved hand to seemingly touch her chin in thought, down to the arrangement of her hair and russet colored bonnet over a matching walking coat and trim, shined black boots. From the angled tilt of her face, he could see a slight smile. She was enjoying this.

"What?" he asked.

"So rude, Horatio," she murmured. "So, is your pretty friend as charming as I?"

"Would you believe me if I said yes?"

Her smile withered. "No." The smile was back, brighter this time.

"What is it, Lucinda?"

"Nothing. I just wanted to see if you'd come when I called." She giggled.

His face burned. He'd fallen for her tricks, and not for the first time. He turned and began to walk away.

"Horatio?" she called.

He stopped.

"I miss you," Lucinda said.

He looked back, taking in the sight of her fair skin, unblemished by the sun. Soft blush pink lips that ached to be kissed, cheeks rosy. Her light-blue eyes glimmered with anticipation. It was the same look she'd had before a performance at the theater, or before they'd made love. He knew it well. He couldn't identify his feelings. Anger and hurt warred with longing and an urge to rip the bonnet from her head, run his hands through her luxuriously thick hair and pull her to him, bringing her face to his. He'd done it before; he could do it again. And from the confident look in her eyes, she knew it too.

She licked her lips in anticipation. "Horatio?"

He walked away.

Emmeline stood by looking at paintings when Mr. Whittaker rejoined her. He stood by Emmeline's side, not saying a word.

"Everything all right?" she asked quietly.

"Fine," he said. "An old acquaintance of mine wanted a word." He smiled at that. Lucinda would shudder and rant at being called old.

"Just an acquaintance, or...?" she hedged.

He looked at her. "It is no business of yours."

She raised an eyebrow. "As the woman you are courting and in a business arrangement with, I think I should know about these things.

If there is another woman in the picture, I'd like to know."

Their eyes met and it was like meeting hot steel. Her eyes blazed.

"You're jealous," he realized aloud.

"I'm not." Two spots of color appeared in her cheeks.

"You are." He smiled.

"Nonsense. Why would I be jealous? You're only walking away with a married woman," she said.

He looked sternly at her. "We are old acquaintances. You have nothing to worry about."

"I'm not worried." She frowned and looked away, then met his eyes. "I mean, I trust you. If you say there is nothing between you, then I believe you."

"Believe what?" Charlotte asked, approaching them. "I say, is Mrs. Bryant formerly the actress Lucinda Cross? I thought she looked familiar. Is she a friend of yours, Mr. Whittaker?"

"You could say that," he said. "Are you a patron of the arts?"

"I do like the theater, I must admit. It was a guilty pleasure of ours when my Anthony was still alive." She smiled. "Could you make an introduction? I'd love to meet her."

He winced inwardly. "I would rather—"

"Charlotte, he doesn't wish to."

"Oh please, Mr. Whittaker. Do it as a favor to me, won't you? I'm such an admirer of hers. You'll do it, won't you?" Charlotte asked.

"Charlotte," Emmeline began.

"I would be happy to," he mumbled, bowed, and walked in the direction of Lucinda, who had been watching their exchange.

"What is it, Horatio? Back already? Don't tell me, you missed me, too," she said.

"Mrs. Harcourt wishes to make your acquaintance," he said gruffly.

"Hah, no thank you. I have all the friends I need."

Lucinda threw a hand in the air and began to turn her back, when he added, "She is a great admirer of yours. From your theater days."

The change in her personality was instant. The wicked sneer disappeared and was replaced with a magnanimous smile. "Of course, I would be delighted to meet her. Please, do make the introduction." She took his arm, wrapping her gloved hands around his bicep.

He inhaled the scent of her floral perfume. He hated himself for breathing in the scent, and worse, enjoying it. He hated how it made him feel.

She played the lovely, charming actress and immediately gave the women a sweet smile. Emmeline was polite and cordial, while Charlotte seemed excited at meeting such a well-known actress and fawned over her. Lucinda loved the attention and was flattered and laughed, as making charming conversation was her skill.

Horatio stood by, bored, but couldn't leave without being rude. He bit his tongue and frowned at Lucinda's firm grip on his arm. It felt proprietary.

He looked up to see Emmeline's eyes on him, and how they flickered to Lucinda's gloved hand on his arm. He met her gaze, and felt disturbed when she excused herself to look at the paintings nearby.

Horatio smiled as Lucinda tutted. "Well, that was rude."

Charlotte faltered and said, "Don't mind her, she really loves art. Now tell me, are you performing again anytime soon?"

Horatio lowered his arm and twisted slightly, forcing Lucinda to remove her hand. He ignored her small noise of protest and went after Emmeline.

He approached her and like a silent shadow, stood by her side. Being taller, he got a whiff of her perfume. This wasn't floral at all, but held a hint of spice. He decided he liked it. It suited her, much like her temperament.

He murmured by her ear, "Everything all right?"

She jumped, surprised at seeing him so close. "Yes. Of course. Sorry, you startled me."

He stuck his hands in his pockets and stepped closer. "And are you as impressed by her as your sister-in-law?"

A delicate snort was his answer. He followed her gaze to the painting, a landscape in oil of wild animals and men at the hunt. To the wild look in the beasts' eyes as they knew they were being hunted, he felt he could relate.

"She seems to be a good friend of yours," Emmeline said.

"We were friends, once upon a time. Now we are just nodding acquaintances."

"That's all?"

He turned to her and pulled her behind a large sculpture.

"What are you—" she started when he took her chin in his hands.

"Miss Harcourt," he said, looking her in the eyes. They were brown.

"Yes?" she said quietly.

"Trust me. I am only courting you. I will not have eyes for any other woman but you. I trust you will do me the same courtesy."

She nodded, her eyes never leaving his.

Approaching footsteps alerted them of voices nearby. He let go of her chin and dropped his hands.

She looked around and then dropped her gaze to the floor.

"What's wrong? Don't you trust me?" he asked, taking her hand.

"It is not her trust you need to be worried about," Charlotte snapped, shocking them both. She stood there beside Mrs. Bryant, her face cold. "Emmeline, get away from him."

CHAPTER SIX

E MMELINE ALLOWED CHARLOTTE to lead her away. They made no apologies or excuses to Mrs. Bryant or Mr. Whittaker, and took a carriage home. As soon as they were back inside their townhouse, Charlotte tore off her bonnet, her black bonnet ribbons getting tangled in her gloved fingers as she rounded on Emmeline. "I cannot believe you would carry on that way. What were you thinking?"

"We were just talking, Charlotte."

"Poppycock. Easy for you to say. I know how it starts. A few smiles, some pretty words in your ear and then we find you in the hayloft again, your arms wrapped around him like a wanton whore."

Emmeline stared at her sister-in-law; her breath caught. Charlotte had never lashed out at her like this before. Was it her grief talking? She took off her bonnet and walking coat and trying for decorum, her heart beating in her throat, she hung up her coat with trembling fingers. She faced her sister-in-law. "I am not a whore."

Charlotte followed Emmeline into the drawing room and slammed the door shut behind her, making Emmeline jump. "I had thought you were taken advantage of back in Bedford, when your brother first told me of your troubles. But now I see for myself that you were talking in private corners with a new man, like some secretive... hussy," Charlotte practically spat.

"I am not a hussy," Emmeline said. "And you don't have to worry about me."

"Don't I? It was your brother's concern for your safety that first alerted me to this. I thought you were innocent, but you can't help yourself, can you?" Charlotte asked.

"Excuse me? I'm sorry, but who do you think you are? We may be related by marriage, but you are not my mother, father, or brother," Emmeline said.

"That's right. I'm your sister-in-law, the one who took you in when your family threw you out after they found out what you'd done. You think your brother took you in out of the kindness of his heart? Don't make me laugh." Charlotte's dark eyes were like daggers.

Emmeline stared at her.

"It was my doing, Emmeline. Mine. If I hadn't stepped in and urged him to take you here to stay with us, you would have been out on the street. Or sent to a nunnery. So accept your blessings and show a little concern for propriety and my feelings, Emmeline. I may be a widow, but I have eyes. I can see the way you were looking at him."

"I wasn't—"

"Don't lie."

"We were just talking. We are courting, Charlotte."

Charlotte raised her pretty eyebrows. "Is that so? Funny, he did not ask my permission or send word to your parents. I would have thought he would do us the courtesy, but I see that, just as ever, you have chosen a man who cares little for propriety—if he is the sort who steals you away around corners for private chats."

"That is unfair."

"You are just lucky that it was only Mrs. Bryant there to see you. I cannot bear to think what would have happened had more people seen."

"Seen what, Charlotte? A couple talking? We are courting. There is nothing wrong with that."

Charlotte's eyes narrowed. "You almost made fools of this family once, Emmeline. You will not do it again. Not under my roof."

"What is that supposed to mean?"

"My goodwill only goes so far. I loved your brother and wanted to offer you some Christian charity after your plight. But do not test me, Emmeline. I beg you, do not."

Emmeline held her tongue. She had a fiery temper when provoked, but she also knew a line when she saw one. "Are you threatening to kick me out?"

Charlotte looked at her sister-in-law and her expression softened. "I would never. We are family." She quieted and folded her hands in her lap. "But I would remind you of your duty to your family. To conduct yourself with honor and decorum. To be ladylike and to have a care for your person and remember how it looks, when you are in the company of men."

Emmeline looked at her. Her shoulders slumped. "I am... sorry." She walked over and sat on one of the two sofas in the room, resting against it for comfort. "I thought it was obvious when Mr. Whittaker called earlier, that he was intending to court me. When he invited us out, and... we met at the Lyon's Den, and he suggested it there."

"Suggested courting you? Lord, you make it sound like a business transaction."

It rather was, Emmeline thought.

"Never mind. When he calls here again, I will ask him his intentions and write to your father and mother. They deserve to know." Charlotte thought, with a smile, "I shall write and tell them we met the famous actress, Lucinda Cross."

Emmeline frowned.

"I can delay my letter if you wish."

"It is not that."

"Then what?"

"I do not think Mrs. Bryant was very friendly."

"Stuff and nonsense, she was the picture of friendliness. Very amiable, and very good of her to talk to people like us."

Emmeline did not share her sister-in-law's admiration for actors. "I met her already. I didn't know then that she was a former actress, I just thought she was Mrs. Bryant."

"I can't believe you wouldn't recognize her. She is a jewel. A gem. She—"

"Was unkind toward Mr. Whittaker."

"I cannot believe that. Why would she be? Surely you are mistaken. They are old friends, I'm sure."

Emmeline shrugged. "I think they used to be, but are more just acquaintances now."

"Hm. Let us ask Mr. Whittaker when we next see him. When do you think he will call again?"

Emmeline's mouth quirked into a smile. "I'm not so sure, considering the way we left."

"Oh, yes. Well, think of it as a test. If he still comes by, you'll know he likes you," Charlotte said, and went off in search of tea.

Emmeline went to her room, closed the door, and sat down on her small narrow bed, resting her hands on her knees.

Mr. Whittaker seemed honest, but could she trust him? She hardly trusted herself, and what with Charlotte's rude reaction to their private conversation, she could only guess as to how it looked. Would he decide to end their business arrangement? And what *was* Mrs. Bryant's behavior toward him all about? At first it seemed like she had a ready familiarity with him, almost like a lover. Then she had looked upon them with distaste, only to be charming a moment later at their formal introduction. It was odd.

THE NEXT DAY she opened the shop and sold a few hats, but no umbrellas, as the weather was fine. The sun shone outside, which offered a great spotlight to the lovely bonnets and hats Emmeline had set upon stands in the window. Like jewels in the sun, the smart bonnets with pink silk, white satin, and straw with colorful ribbons shone, and by lunchtime, she had sold all three from the display.

Emmeline smiled as she wrapped up the packages and handed them to the patrons, placing a delicate business card in each striped hat box. It was a pleasure to see women enjoy themselves, whether they amused themselves with a spur of the moment purchase, or to see their eyes dance at the sight of a turban or bonnet made of straw, which paired with a pink or blue ribbon, would look lovely at a walk in the park. She gave a little sigh of happiness and stood back as the most recent customer left, chatting with a friend.

But then the bell rang, signaling the entrance of a new customer, and she put on her best smile, which faltered in an instant. Mr. and Mrs. Bryant entered, looking very full of themselves. Today, Mrs. Bryant wore a green walking coat over a light yellow dress with light green gloves, and a green hat with a wide yellow ribbon. It matched, sort of, but one look at the hat and Emmeline could see it was poorly made. The hatmaker had substituted substance for style, and while it looked pretty enough, the ribbon was already slipping, and the hat's green satin did not look very sturdy. In short, it looked as though the hat might deconstruct at any moment. Not that Mrs. Bryant noticed.

She was far too interested to walk around the shop, touching the hats, feathers, gloves, and parasols, tracing a line on the tables to inspect them for dust, as she approached Emmeline. "Why hello, Miss Harcourt. I heard this was your shop. When dear Logan told me you worked in a shop I couldn't believe my ears, but here you are. As your landlady, I simply had to come and inspect the premises." She smiled.

Logan looked bored beside her. "Sell much today?"

"A few things," Emmeline said. "Good morning, Mr. Bryant. Mrs. Bryant." She curtsied, but the favor was not returned.

"It is afternoon," Mr. Bryant pointed out, checking his timepiece.

"So it is." Emmeline refused to say more. She wanted to say, "My mistake," but didn't dare. She did not want to give an inch of submission to these people. Not a jot.

"Did you want a hat?" Logan asked his wife.

"I'll look and see."

"Don't dawdle. I'll be outside." He left.

Mrs. Bryant made a show of looking around the shop, picking up hats and examining them, or holding up gloves in the light. She touched most things in the window display and succeeded in disarranging all of them within minutes.

"How is your husband, Mrs. Bryant?" Emmeline asked.

"He is well. As you saw. Why?"

"I wondered how he must be feeling after his fall the other night, outside Mrs. Dove-Lyon's home."

Mrs. Bryant's eyes flicked up to Emmeline. "He is very well. A little tired perhaps. Although I must say, if anyone should be worried, it must be you. Are you quite well?"

"Yes."

"The reason I ask is because of your sudden departure yesterday. It took us by surprise. Mr. Whittaker was quite offended. It wouldn't surprise me in the least if he did not wish to speak to you or see you again."

Emmeline swallowed and bowed her head. "I am sorry to have given offense."

"Oh, it is no trouble to me. I was not offended. Your dear Charlotte was only looking after you, and quite right too. But... tell me. Is it true that you and Mr. Whittaker are courting?"

"Yes. I gather you two know each other."

"Oh, yes. Very well. We have enjoyed a long and close friendship these past few years." Mrs. Bryant's pretty mouth curved into a smile, but it did not meet her eyes. "A word of advice, Miss Harcourt. I would keep a distance from Mr. Whittaker. He has been crossed in love and well... He has loved another woman for a long time. Whatever romantic notions or affections he has shown you, whatever promises he makes, believe me, they are not genuine."

Emmeline stared at her. "What do you mean?"

Lucinda touched her chest in a dramatic motion, worthy of the stage. "I do not speak for myself, only to be honest with you, woman to woman. I am doing you a favor. You ought to know. He loves another. He may try and distract himself with you, but it will only end in heartbreak. You should know this before you end up falling for him."

"I see. And how would you know this? Who is the woman?"

Lucinda tapped her nose. "I am one of his oldest friends, as is my husband. We know Horatio far better than anyone else." She shrugged. "Take my advice, or not, Miss Harcourt. I simply mean for you to be forewarned, is all. I'd hate to see you throw yourself away on a man who is not emotionally available."

She turned just as the door opened to reveal—

"Why, Horatio, what are you doing here? And Mrs. Harcourt, what a pleasure."

Mr. Whittaker and her sister-in-law entered the shop, curtsied, and bowed to Lucinda. Mr. Whittaker looked at her, then at Emmeline, who blushed.

"Mrs. Bryant, what a pleasant surprise. Oh, do tell me you've come to look at our hats," Charlotte said, coming forward to talk to her.

As they chatted, Mr. Whittaker found his way to Emmeline, who suddenly took great interest in arranging a set of hat pins by the till.

"Miss Harcourt?" he asked. "How are you today?"

"I am well, thank you. And you?"

"Tolerable. Better now."

She looked up and met his eyes, saw his slight smile. She smiled back, briefly, and relaxed her hands. "I am sorry we left the way we did."

"Are you all right?"

She nodded. "Perfectly well. I... do you still wish to continue with our arrangement?"

He blinked. "Do you not?"

She swallowed. "I do, it's just...." She blushed. "After yesterday, I thought perhaps you would not want to. You might rather not wish to be seen with me."

"If that is what you think, then you are mistaken," he said firmly.

"Then you are not offended?" she asked.

"No. Not at all. I came to your townhouse to ask your sister-in-law if I might have permission to court you."

"Oh." Emmeline exhaled. "What did she say?"

"She wasn't sure at first, but once I gave her the bouquet of flowers I'd brought for you, she agreed. In fact she demanded to accompany me here, so that we might all take a walk in the park together."

"A walk? How wonderful. I'll bring Logan along," Mrs. Bryant said, a smile on her face. "I do so love a walk."

"You do?" Mr. Whittaker asked her.

"Of course I do. Silly man," Mrs. Bryant said. "Come, let us go together." She took his arm and led the way outside.

Charlotte approached Emmeline. "Mr. Whittaker came by this morning with flowers. He'd come to see you and asked permission to court you. I said yes. I trust that is acceptable?"

Emmeline nodded. "Thank you."

"He seems kind enough. And I suppose if I am chaperoning, then there will be no mischief, so it will keep us both out of trouble." She smiled. "Let us go. You can shut up the shop for an hour. The fresh air will do you good."

Emmeline agreed, and shut up the shop, joining the others outside. They walked along New Bond Street and down Bruton Street to Berkeley Square, where they made a smart little party along the walkways. The grass was green and lush, ducks and geese waddled past, and trees offered shade and whispered in the wind as the sun shone overhead, giving a warm light.

Things seemed pleasant, with Charlotte waving at the welcome sight of Mrs. Dove-Lyon strolling up ahead, a mysterious sight swathed in a black walking dress, hat, and veil. Mr. and Mrs. Bryant were not far behind, followed by Mr. Whittaker and Emmeline. Everything seemed like the makings of a good day, when Emmeline spotted a man standing by a tree, watching them. When the light hit his face, she stopped and stared.

"What is it?" Mr. Whittaker asked. "Are you all right?"

"I'm fine." Emmeline kept walking.

"You are not. Your face is pale. You look like you've seen a ghost," he said.

"What is the matter? Emmeline, are you unwell?" Charlotte came to her side, followed by Mrs. Dove-Lyon, who nodded hello and expressed concern for Emmeline's health.

Emmeline hated being at the center of attention. "I'm fine, I promise. It is just the sun. I... feel a bit faint. Forgive me. I am well enough. Let us continue walking, please."

Mr. Whittaker offered her his arm, which she took. She took comfort in the solid hardness of his arm, finding solace in its steady weight.

But not five minutes passed before she spotted him again, closer this time. She was not the only one to take notice.

"I say, do you know that man?" Mr. Whittaker asked. "He seems to be following us."

"What man?" Emmeline asked. But a note in her voice betrayed her.

"Miss Harcourt?" Mr. Whittaker asked. "What is wrong?" He stopped and faced her, his eyes searching hers. "What is it? You can tell me."

She paused, feeling her heart flutter like a butterfly. "I... that is..."

A gunshot fired and clipped Mr. Bryant, who fell and clapped a hand to his ear. "Aaahh!"

"Darling!" Lucinda went to his side.

Emmeline fainted.

CHAPTER SEVEN

E MMELINE WOKE TO find herself being jostled. A whiff of men's cologne hit her nose. She breathed and her eyes fluttered open. "What? What is going on? What is—"

"She's awake." The jostling stopped.

She opened her eyes to see the concerned face of Mr. Whittaker looking down at her. "Miss Harcourt, are you all right?"

"What happened?"

"Mr. Bryant was struck by a stray bullet and has taken ill. You fainted from the shock of it. I am taking you home."

"No, I am fine." She realized her surroundings. "Are you... Am I?" She raised her head to find he held her in his arms. "Mr. Whittaker, please. Do let me down."

He stopped. "Are you certain?"

"Yes, please. I can walk." She touched his arm.

Their eyes met, and he slowly let her down. Once her feet touched the earth, she wobbled. His hands were instantly around her waist, steadying her.

Charlotte reached for her. "Emmeline, what happened? I've never seen you faint before."

"Too much sun, I think. And the shock. How is Mr. Bryant? Was he badly hurt?"

"It appears to be a flesh wound. Two gentlemen were examining a gun and it went off; it just happened to graze him. We're just lucky a good Samaritan happened to be nearby. He called a carriage and sent Mr. and Mrs. Bryant on their way home."

"Oh?"

"Yes, some fellow who happened to be walking near us. He heard the gunshot and saw you faint, and we all worried you might have been hit," said Mr. Whittaker. "Charlotte inspected you and declared you were not, so I took the liberty of carrying you."

She realized the source of the jostling: he had been carrying her out of the park and to the entrance. People stopped and watched as their group approached the carriages that hung about for hire.

He handed her to Charlotte and raised an arm for the nearest carriage. She saw him ignore Charlotte's hand and instead help her inside the carriage, handing her in. Once satisfied, he shut the door, paid the driver, and sent them on their way.

As a new source of jostling began, Charlotte repeated her question. "Emmeline, are you all right? Shall I call for a doctor?"

"No, I'm fine. Honestly."

"What made you faint like that?"

"The sun, I think," Emmeline said.

"Are you sure? I have heard that the London air is dirty and not at all good for a young person's health. If you want, I can write to your father tonight and send you back to Bedford. What do you think?"

Emmeline did not want to leave the shop, or Mr. Whittaker. A part of her enjoyed his attention, even if was all a sham. But what of Nicholas? Had it been him? And if she did tell Charlotte, what would be her reaction? Would she send her away?

She had her own problems to deal with. Without her, the shop would flounder. Mr. Bryant would run roughshod over them, and it would fold in no time at all. Besides, Charlotte was still grieving her brother, and she did not wish to add to her burden. Telling her would make it seem like she was not to be trusted, or worse, that she could not solve her own problems by herself.

"I'm fine; don't worry. I just need a drink and to rest a little," Emmeline said.

As they drew closer to home, Emmeline's mind was made up. She would deal with Nicholas and say not a word of this to anyone. She was a grown woman of twenty-two years. She ran a successful hat shop in London and was being courted by a gentleman. She could handle a man from her past.

But she did not sleep well that night, nor the next. She began to see Nicholas everywhere. On the road, walking along in crowds, at church, and outside the park. But as if seeing him put him in her mind, she was filled with shame and humiliation at the memory of their last moment together, in Bedford.

It had started innocently enough. She had tripped in the aisle coming out of a pew at church and he had caught her and helped her up. His warm hand on her waist and back, their eyes had met, and she had felt a jolt, as if he had awakened something she'd never known was asleep inside her.

They exchanged nods at the next church service and smiles at the following one. It got so that she found reasons to dally after the service and as it just so happened, he was walking in the same direction. He was not well-read or intellectual, but he had a way of speaking that made you listen and pay attention, and he was smart. World-smarts, she supposed he had. But that wasn't all that attracted her.

His face, so handsome. His voice when he talked was like honey. He had dirty blonde hair that needed a cut and hung like a mop over his eyes. With light brown eyes and a square chin, with tanned golden skin and a winsome smile, she felt drawn to him like a moth to a flame. And in no time at all, their little clandestine meetings became something more.

They began courting in private. When she questioned the need for secrecy, Nicholas said it was because he was a poor farmer, and her family would not approve. She said as they were both families in trade, she did not see the harm, but he refused. He said if she said anything, he would deny everything and stop seeing her. So she played along.

He'd drawn her into the barn he worked at and led her off into the shadows where they kissed, he'd trailed his fingers down her neck, and laid on top of her, letting her feel the weight of a man's body. She reveled in his touch, and if she minded the smell of hay, horse, and manure that clung to his clothes, she did not say so. This was a new experience, a man touching her. She felt awakened, and wanted more. Dreamed of more.

But then they were caught. Found out. By the man who owned the farm, who took her by the arm, ripped her away from Nicholas and fired him on the spot. The farmer sent her home with a flea in her ear, and said out of courtesy to her family, he would not speak of this.

Nicholas, however, was another matter. A day passed, then two. He was not at church, and she worried and wondered about him. Would she ever hear from him again? Did he love her?

But then after walking home from the market in town she entered the family house and found him sitting in their drawing room, as if he belonged there. Gone was his pleasant expression, his warm smile. His eyes had narrowed and looked her over without a second glance, and the tilt of his chin revealed a smirk, a sneer, and something altogether different. He was different from the man she'd known and fallen for.

Her mother was pale, her father's face pinched with anxiety. She had sat by them and wondered what was going on.

Her father sat rigid with anger. "Why do you think Mr. Runcorn is here, Emmeline? Have you lain with this man?"

"No. That is, I do not think so," she said, turning red.

Her father ran a hand through his thinning hair.

"Mr. Runcorn, have you come to make me an offer? Of marriage?" Emmeline asked.

Nicholas laughed, a harsh sound.

"No, he has not. He has come to extort money from us," her father said.

"What?"

"Oh, we've lain together all right. Your daughter's a right cow for it. Can't get enough of me. You should have heard her calling out in the barn for more. 'Oh Nicholas,'" he mimicked.

Emmeline turned pale. "Nicholas."

"He is Mr. Runcorn to you, girl," her father growled.

"What do you want?" Emmeline asked.

Nicholas smirked. "Money."

"You don't want me?"

His silence was her answer.

"But why?"

And then it came out. This had been his goal all along. She'd been nothing but a girl to dally with.

The realization hit her as hard as if she'd been physically struck. The man she'd fallen for, who'd ensnared her with his easy smiles and jokes and wandering hands, was no more than a blackguard, a rake, a swindler. A man who enjoyed toying with men's daughters and then extorting them for money, in return for keeping their reputations intact.

She blinked hard but barely moved a muscle. "But I don't understand. We never, I mean we didn't... I am still a maid." Emotion heated her voice.

"Hah! Like anyone will believe that," Nicholas said. "And no one will once I tell 'em. Unless you pay."

The blood drained from Emmeline's face, and she fled the room, followed by her mother. She wept on her bed and took no comfort from her mother's warm hand on her back. When she heard the front door open and close, she came back into the drawing room.

Her father told her the news directly; he had paid the man and accepted his account of events, for that was all that anyone would believe. In a man's world, it would be Mr. Runcorn's word against hers, and no one would believe a girl who said she was a virgin when it was likely she was not. She would be leaving in the morning, to visit her brother and his new wife in London.

"For how long?"

"Indefinitely. Until we can be sure that you have not ruined us all," came the hard answer.

She loved her parents, but this was too much to bear. They had done well financially and had money, but for her to dally with a farmer and fall prey to his false charms, the damage to all their reputations would be great. Better that she go.

"Papa?"

"I do not want to see you right now. Give my best to your brother and his wife," her father spoke the words without even looking at her. He stood there by the window, watching the man who had taken all her happiness and ruined it within an afternoon walk away and out of their lives, forever.

Until now.

That had been five and a half years ago. She was smarter now, older. And harder than she'd been at age seventeen. She would never again let herself be fooled into trusting another man with her heart. Not ever. She would smile and pretend to fall for Mr. Whittaker's charms, but she would never lose her heart again. Her family and her own reputation meant too much to her to throw it all away.

She set up the shop window, unaware of what she was doing. In no time at all, she had served customers, each arrival and departure signaled by the sound of the bell. With each one she smiled, sold hats or gloves, or took orders, and acted as though nothing was wrong. But she was distracted.

"Are you all right?" came Mr. Whittaker's voice from behind her. She turned. "Oh, hello."

"Miss Harcourt, I have said your name twice already, and you have rearranged that hat display three times in the last five minutes I have been here. Please, stop a moment." He wore a smart brown suit jacket and matching trousers with a light vanilla colored waistcoat and a gold pocket watch that caught the light. A white cravat had been swiftly tied, but still gave a stiff and polite look, much like himself. His chin was freshly shaven, and his eyes were full of worry.

Part of her shyly wished to run her hands through his dark curls, and she stopped herself by rubbing her hands against her hips. She stepped away from the display and walked back to the counter. "I am well, as you see."

"You are not. Something has distracted you. What is it? Maybe I can help."

She shook her head. This was her problem, not his. "No, I am fine, honestly."

"Are you certain? You don't seem well."

She gave him a sunny smile. "I am quite well."

He didn't believe her, she could tell, but he played along. "In that case, I am here to offer you an invitation. To the theater. I have procured a box and thought perhaps you and your sister-in-law might like to come along."

"Oh, I—"

"They would be delighted, I am sure," Mrs. Dove-Lyon said, coming closer. "Forgive me for interrupting, my dear, but I was just coming to place an order for a hat, and I couldn't help but overhear. The rumors are true, then, you two really are courting. How delightful."

Emmeline smiled thinly. She hadn't even realized they weren't alone.

"We are," Mr. Whittaker said. He touched his hat. "Until this evening then, Miss Harcourt. Meet me outside the Drury Lane Theater at six o'clock."

"A splendid idea. Good day, Mr. Whittaker," Mrs. Dove-Lyon said. She waited until Mr. Whittaker had left the shop, before she said, "So. Tell me how it's going. I want to hear everything about you and Mr. Whittaker."

Emmeline felt false. "It is just a sham, Mrs. Dove-Lyon. We are courting only in pretense. We don't hold any true feelings for each other."

Mrs. Dove-Lyon's face fell behind her slightly translucent black veil. "I am sorry to hear it. He has not had a happy time of life, and I had hoped that your romance would make him happy. He has seemed so for the first time in a long time. Or at least, not so stiff and formal as is his wont."

Emmeline smiled, a little. "Perhaps that personality trait is what attracted us to each other. We are both possessed of a pensive, obstinate nature."

Mrs. Dove-Lyon snorted. "I think there is more to it than that. I have known him for some time, and he has barely given any of the pretty young women at the Den a second glance." She paused. "Are you sure he holds no deeper feelings for you? When you fainted yesterday, did he not carry you?"

"I woke up to find he was, yes." Emmeline blushed. She could still smell the hint of his cologne.

Mrs. Dove-Lyon raised a delicate eyebrow. "And here he is a day later, to enquire after your health and invite you and your sister-in-law out. Do you truly doubt his feelings for you?"

"Of course. He is just playing the part of the concerned beau, that's all."

"And how are you feeling after your fall? You did seem rather pale."

"I'm fine. Please, let us discuss something else." While Emmeline took down the order for a fine hat in black satin and matching gloves for Mrs. Dove-Lyon, she asked, "Have you heard anything about Mr. Bryant? After the incident yesterday, I mean."

"No. Only that the bullet grazed him, and he's been in foul spirits ever since. Although, knowing that man, that is no change from his regular mood. He simply has a reason for it now." Mrs. Dove-Lyon smiled impishly.

"Was it an accident?"

"I couldn't say. I paid a call to Mrs. Bryant, but she was looking after him and wasn't receiving callers. I would say the attack was accidental, although it is strange. It is a public park. There are the carriages, and horses, but no shooting, and hunts aren't allowed on the grounds. What anyone would be doing with a pistol, I do not know."

That day after the shop closed, Emmeline decided to pay a call on Mr. and Mrs. Bryant. She'd learned where they lived from Mrs. Dove-Lyon and decided to take a pair of gloves as a small gift.

At first, she was not going to be admitted, but when she said she had a small gift for Mrs. Bryant, she was shown inside to a small parlor. She was not invited to sit, nor was she offered tea or a biscuit, and instead stood, looking around the room. The room itself was darkly lit, with meager candles and a sooty fireplace that needed cleaning.

The sofa cushions were tattered and worn, as was the threadbare carpet she stood on. The curtains looked old and drafty with moth holes, and the windows needed washing. In short, the room was dirty. But she knew the Bryants to be wealthy, so where was all the money going?

Mrs. Bryant entered the room, wearing a red dress that looked to be made of silk. Its cut and trimmings were fanciful and expensive looking, as were her elaborate hairstyle and makeup. "What do you want? Come to ask for an extension of your rent?" she asked with a smile.

"Good afternoon, Mrs. Bryant. And no, I've come to call and see how Mr. Bryant is doing. I also brought you a pair of gloves I thought you might like." She passed over the small, delicately packaged parcel.

Lucinda Bryant tore it open, shredding the paper to fall to the floor. Her mouth withered at the sight of the gloves. "Gray wool? What am I to do with these? It's a warm October. I'll roast like a pig in them." She tossed them to the nearest sofa. "Why are you really here?"

"How is your husband?"

"Mr. Whittaker boring you already, is he?"

"I…" Emmeline balked.

"Oh, don't play the coy maid with me. What do you want with my husband?"

Emmeline stared at Mrs. Bryant and decided to come clean. "I overheard your husband complaining about some threats earlier, a few days ago, and then what with the carriage incident and now this, I wonder if someone is trying to hurt him."

Mrs. Bryant surveyed Emmeline boldly and crossed her arms over her chest. "You fancy yourself somewhat of a member of the watch, do you?"

"No, not at all. But if I can help, I will. I just wanted to see if he was all right, considering. It must have been an awful fright," Emmeline said.

"It certainly was for you. It's not every girl who faints at the sound of a gunshot. Why did you faint?"

"I don't know. It scared me, I suppose."

"You faint at the sound of a gun, and yet you come over here, under the pretext of a gift, to wheedle your way into our home and to offer yourself as a person to look into these matters." Mrs. Bryant's voice held a mocking note. "What a joke. Get out."

Emmeline said, "I meant no offense."

"I'll be the judge of that. Now leave, before I call the watch on you. My husband will not be pleased to learn you came here."

"Who's there, Lucinda?" Logan Bryant's voice called down.

"No one, dear. Just a busybody," Mrs. Bryant said with a wicked smile.

Emmeline left, feeling lower than before. At another time she would have argued with Mrs. Bryant, but to do so while a guest was beyond rude, and she felt like her confidence had fallen in recent days.

That night she dressed with care. She and Charlotte ate an early dinner. Charlotte looked resplendent in black satin with panels of mauve and gauzy, black sheer fabric overlaid, and Emmeline wore a pretty light pink dress with an embroidered ribbon at the high waist. She wore light pink gloves and a ribbon in her hair, with a thin gold necklace at her throat. She wore no makeup aside from a touch of rouge at her cheeks and lips, and a dark aubergine cloak for warmth.

The October night was chilly, and they took a carriage from Cheapside to Drury Lane, joining a queue of people going to the theater. As they approached the main entrance, there was a crush of people going inside, and they just caught sight of Mr. Whittaker. Holding hands so as not to get separated, they found him and bid him hello.

There was little space to bow, much less move, so he exchanged social niceties with them both and shook hands with Miss Harcourt.

"Come, come, let us go. I had forgotten how much I dislike crowds," he said.

Once safe and secure in the box he had purchased, they sat as he procured glasses of wine for them. As the play began, Emmeline felt a pair of eyes on her. She looked around but did not see anything.

"Is everything all right, Miss Harcourt?" Mr. Whittaker asked, near her ear.

"Yes, fine, thanks." She sat and looked straight ahead, keeping her attention on the play. It was a comedy, designed to make the audience amused with cheap jokes and overexaggerated puns. There was a modicum of story, but she had trouble focusing and when the interval came, she rose, wanting to stretch her legs.

"What a sorry excuse for theater. I've never seen such a terrible production," Mr. Whittaker said. "I'm sorry, ladies, I've never seen this one before. It came recommended, but now I won't trust that source again."

"That's all right. It's not terrible. Certainly entertaining," Emmeline said. "If you'll excuse me, I'll stretch my legs a little." She curtsied and disappeared out the door.

Once in the corridors, there were people everywhere, swarming like ants. It felt even busier than the outside had been, and it wasn't long before she bumped into people as a matter of course.

"Oh." She bumped into a woman and said, "Oh, I'm sorry."

"You should be. Watch where you're going." The woman turned around. "Oh, it's you."

Mrs. Bryant eyed Emmeline's gown from top to bottom, a small smirk on her face.

"Miss Harcourt, there you are. It's a wonder you didn't get lost," Mr. Whittaker said, coming up behind her.

"Hello, Horatio," Mrs. Bryant said with a winning smile.

"Mrs. Bryant. We were just going back to our seats. Miss Harcourt?" He held out an arm.

She took it, when Mrs. Bryant said, "What a pity, for I was just making a new acquaintance. One I think you know, Miss Harcourt."

"Oh?"

"Yes, indeed. This young man says he is well acquainted with you and your family. What was your name again?" She tapped a man on the shoulder from a foot away.

He turned, and Emmeline's blood froze in her veins.

"Nicholas," he said, eyeing her up and down. "Nicholas Runcorn."

Chapter Eight

H ORATIO DIDN'T LIKE this new arrival, not one bit.

"Hello, Emmy," the unfamiliar man said.

Emmeline paled and her mouth dropped open. It was as if she had been struck dumb.

"Who is this?" Horatio asked, stood in front of Emmeline, ready to shield her.

"Nicholas Runcorn," the man introduced himself. "Hello, Emmy. I've been looking for you." He smiled at Emmeline.

"You two know each other?" Horatio asked.

"Oh yes, we've known each other for years. Back in Bedford," Mr. Runcorn said with a grin.

Horatio stared. Who was this man who had such an effect on her?

"You're... you're here," she uttered.

"Yes." The man's answering smile was far too self-satisfied. With his every grin Emmeline seemed to grow weaker and shrink into herself.

Horatio put a warm hand on her lower back, offering her comfort in the touch. She looked at him with relief.

"How nice of you to say hello. Well, Miss Harcourt, we should be getting back. Your sister-in-law shouldn't be kept waiting. Shall we?" Mr. Whittaker held out an arm.

"Sister-in-law? I should like to pay my respects."

"Another time. Enjoy the performance." Horatio gently took Emmeline by the elbow, steered her away from Lucinda and Nicholas, and back toward the box. Once away from them and down the corridor, he pulled her aside. "Are you going to tell me what that was all about?"

"No. It is none of your concern," she said.

He pulled her into a dark recess of the wall, away from the crowd passing by, and he gently grasped her chin, tilting it up so she met his eyes. He liked the warmth he saw there, even if her expression was laced with fear.

"If we are to court properly, then there can be no secrets between us. You can tell me whatever is wrong. I will listen," he told her.

She pulled away and he let go, his hand instead falling to his side. She looked down and said, "It is nothing."

"It is not. Who is that man and why does his appearance disturb you so? Do you two have an understanding?" he asked.

"No," she said, sharper than was necessary. "No. We do not. We are acquaintances, nothing more."

"You are lying," he said. At the sudden heat in her eyes, he amended, "You are not telling me everything. I would like to hear it."

She shook her head. "No. It is not your problem."

"Miss Harcourt, how many beaus have you had?" he asked.

She blinked. "I... One. Maybe. No. Not really. I... none."

"Then I have the advantage, for I have been a lady's beau at least once. What I can tell you is that part of courting, part of being in a relationship, is establishing trust with one another. What bothers you affects me," he said brusquely.

I care. I want to care, if you'll let me, he wanted to say, then stopped himself. What was he thinking? Did he really just almost speak that aloud?

He stiffened. "The offer remains. If this courtship is to succeed, then we need to be honest with each other. I must know about any other gentlemen in the field of play."

"You make it sound like a sport, and my heart is the goal."

"More like the trophy," he said. But so much more than that.

His sports analogy did not go over well, for she scowled. She turned to go back, and he took her hand. He felt a delicate thrill at touching her.

"What?" she asked.

"Tell me. I want to know why that man's presence bothers you."

"Tell me the nature of your relationship with Mrs. Bryant. Tell me your secret and I'll tell you mine," she said.

"Horatio… A word, if you please," Mrs. Bryant's voice carried.

Emmeline snorted, tugged her hand back and said, "When you are ready to share secrets, I will be ready to hear them. Until then, that is the one you seem willing to drop everything for. I wonder if that is who you are really in a relationship with."

"That is not fair," he said.

"Perhaps not. But is it the truth?" She walked back to the box, leaving him standing alone in the corridor.

Mrs. Bryant sailed up to him. "Ah, Horatio. What a delightful little play. I'm enjoying it. Are you?"

"On the contrary, I find the whole thing rather coarse."

"Of course you do. Don't be such a spoilsport. I know you like some of the jokes too. I saw you laughing up there in your box, like some lord of the manor. Although why you're with those two women, I don't know. Why did you bring them? Are you giving your time out of charity now?"

He ignored her jibe. "Miss Harcourt and I are courting, after all."

She laughed. "And where is she? Has she fled from you already?"

He gave her a dirty look.

She simpered and fanned herself with a white lace fan, drawing attention to her chest.

"Don't make trouble," he told her.

Her eyes widened with fake innocence. "Me? I would do nothing of the sort. I only meant to reintroduce old friends. From what I gather, they know each other very well."

He glared at her.

"What? I only speak the truth. Ask her and see if she denies it. She is as virginal as I am." She giggled.

"Stop this."

The corridor was mostly empty. The bell signaling the end of the interval had rung, and the corridor was practically deserted. He looked around. They were alone. He immediately felt uncomfortable.

"Horatio," Mrs. Bryant said, coming closer. Her voice grew soft. "Now that we're alone, I wanted to tell you. I made a mistake."

"What?" He backed against the wall, a picture digging into his side. He coughed and choked on the scent of her heady perfume.

She shifted closer. "I should never have married Logan. I shouldn't have left you at the church waiting for me that day."

He looked at her. She was speaking to his heart. Did he dare listen?

"I... I'm sorry, Horatio. That's what I wanted to say. If I could take our wedding day back and do it differently, I would," she said.

He felt the blood rush from his face. Ice pooled in his veins. He felt cold.

"I should never have let you go. Logan had been after me for months and I felt flattered by the attention. I got distracted. It was silly. I was silly. But I never stopped loving you, Horatio. Never. I still do."

A sliver of pain lanced through his chest. "What are you saying?" he uttered.

Her perfume was cloying. "I miss you. I made a mistake. Can you ever forgive me?"

He looked down at her lovely auburn curls, arranged to dangle at her chest, which was on display in a low-cut crimson gown.

She knew her business and looked up at him with light brown eyes. He'd looked into these so often, he knew them as well as his own. And yet, the words she spoke pained him. What he would have given to hear them, before. But not now.

"Lucinda, I..." He started when she pulled his face toward her into a kiss.

He froze.

Lucinda's lips were plastered to his. His eyes widened as she murmured and held herself to him, pressing her chest into his. He felt the weight, the pressure, and stiffened. She took it as enjoyment and kissed him harder, her tongue seeking his.

A gasp came from nearby. He broke off the kiss.

"Mr. Whittaker?" came the stunned words.

Emmeline stood there, her hand at her mouth. "I'm sorry, I..." She turned and hurried away, back down the corridor.

He groaned and ran a hand through his hair.

"Never mind her. Where were we?" Lucinda asked, reaching for him.

"Stop, Lucinda. Enough." He grasped her by the arms and held her back.

"What?" She stared at him.

"I am not interested in toying with a married woman. Go back to your husband, Lucinda. Save your pretty smiles for him."

Her expression changed from angelic to demonic in an instant. She looked haughty, and balked. "You are rejecting me?"

"Yes."

"Why? I poured my heart out to you. I told you I love you. Don't you love me?" she asked, her soft brown eyes pleading.

"Yes. I do. I did," he clarified. "Once. But not anymore." He tugged at his cravat and looked in the direction Emmeline had run to. "And now you've ruined my courtship with Miss Harcourt."

"Hah. As if that needed any help. It was already on the rocks from what I could see." She took his right hand and pressed it against her chest. "Horatio, I mean it. I love you. I would do anything for you. I would die for you. I would kill for you. I would—"

"Stop this. Don't say such things. It's horrible. I don't want to hear it." He stepped away.

"What if I were single? What if we both were free? Would you have me then?" she asked.

"There is no point in even asking. You are not, we are not. I am courting another woman. You are happily married. That is enough." He bowed. "Good evening, Mrs. Bryant."

She gripped his arm. "I mean it, you know. I would."

He looked at her.

"I'd kill for you. Die for you. Anything, if it meant bringing you back to me," she said.

"Don't talk nonsense, Lucinda. Save the dramatics for the stage."

She dropped his arm like a snake. "I cannot even do that anymore. He won't let me work. Says it's beneath him, and to have a wife as an actress is even worse," she said with disgust.

"I am sorry for you, but that is not my problem." He turned.

"I could make it your problem," she said snidely.

"What?"

She faced him. "I still have the letters you wrote me. The sappy love letters you wrote me when we were courting. What if I were to show him and tell him you were still desirous of me? That you wrote to me in secret and begged for my affection? What would he do then?"

She grinned and unwrapped a lozenge, popping it into her mouth.

"Goodbye, Lucinda. I've had enough of your games." He turned on his heel and walked away, feeling her eyes on him.

But when he returned to the box, his guests were gone. The Misses Harcourt had disappeared. His shoulders slumped and he sat in one of the empty chairs, helping himself to a glass of wine that sat untouched by the seat. He wiped his mouth with his sleeve and looked over at the empty chair where Miss Harcourt had sat.

Damn Lucinda.

She hadn't just gripped his arm as they parted, she had trailed her hand down his arm, leaving him to involuntarily shudder. He hated the effect she had on him, even now, a year later.

He looked across the theater to meet her eyes, but she was already laughing, winking, and cheekily admiring another. Teasing another man, pretending to confide in another woman, adding them all to her little mental notebook of social acquaintances, admirers, and those she could make use of.

Like him, once upon a time.

He'd fallen for her. They'd met at a gallery of paintings, and he was studying a piece when she had commented on it, and warned him away from it. They had both argued and haggled over the artwork they had wanted, and she left with it, but he had an invitation to dinner.

Soon he had bought tickets to her every show, and dragged along his friend, Logan. The three of them became inseparable, laughing, dining, drinking, and entertaining themselves from the final curtain to dawn. She could drink them under the table under the right circumstances, and made sure to laugh and tease anyone present.

It hadn't taken him long to fall in love with her, but once he'd come to realize his feelings, he'd fallen for her hard. And when he declared himself in love, she reciprocated his amour, with passion. Soon they spent days and nights together, to the loss of his soul. He felt those nights where they had drunk champagne and liquor to be soiled, darkened, a wanton excess of money, privilege, depravity, sexuality, and looseness that he never cared to repeat again. What he had thought was saintly, having found a true modern woman with independent thoughts and ideals, he now looked with regret at his actions, at having fallen for an actress who had partied at the expense of his checkbook.

He'd been so oblivious. He'd never even noticed the looks exchanged between her and Logan, nor the missed engagements, the late arrivals. All of it went unnoticed in the days leading up to their wedding.

He remembered standing there at the front of the church, in front of his friends and family, and a collection of her fellow actors and friends from the playhouse. A few minutes' delay had lengthened into something more, until he felt something was wrong.

He'd never expected her to leave him at the altar. To never even show up. And for his best friend Logan to not be there either.

The servants were the ones who had told him. Sometimes if you had to hear bad news, it was better off hearing it straight from a stranger. A stranger's bold words could be cutting and harsh, but they had no ulterior motive, unlike the vague kindness from a person you knew. All attempts to be polite disappeared when he'd called at her lodgings, demanding to know where she was. Had she fallen, had she gotten into trouble, was she all right?

"Miss Cross is perfectly well, sir. She left this morning with her gentleman."

"Her gentleman?" Relief washed over him followed by morbid curiosity. "Who?"

"Mr. Logan Bryant come to take her away. Said they were going to Scotland. Gretna Greene, so that she might escape an unhappy marriage."

Horatio stiffened as if he'd been struck. "Did she seem well? She went willingly? Not under force or duress?"

"No sir. She seemed in a fine mood about it. Made a fuss in ordering the maids to pack her enough traveling trunks for a week, and laughing about the great joke they were to play. When she came back, she told us, we were to call her Mrs. Bryant." He touched his cap and went back inside.

Horatio stood there on the stoop of her home, for how long he did not know. He felt waves of shame, disappointment, rage and anger, humiliation. All these were fleeting, much like her skillful touches between the sheets. They had been bedfellows, nothing more. All this time that he had been courting her, she had dallied with his best friend, and they had run off together. He was nothing more than a lovesick joke.

He felt ill. He walked the streets until fatigued and his feet could no longer carry him; he crumpled at the stone steps of a grand townhouse on Cleveland Row. A burly man told him to clear off, and then reported him to the lady of the house, who came out herself to see the mysterious visitor.

He looked into the veiled eyes of the woman who introduced herself as Mrs. Dove-Lyon, took him inside and gave him a cup of tea, and then something stronger. He sat down on a fine pink settee in her private parlor and told her the story.

She had listened, and when she asked what she could do, he looked at her and said, "Help me forget."

CHAPTER NINE

EMMELINE STOOD OUTSIDE the theater with her cloak wrapped tightly around her as she strode to the nearest hackney carriage that loitered outside. As her sister-in-law went inside, she paid the man and gave him directions to their home, then climbed inside and shut the door with a slam. She tapped the roof and off they went, Emmeline glaring into the darkness.

"What is it, Emmy? Why did we have to leave?" Charlotte asked.

"I wanted to go. I... do not feel well," she mumbled.

"I can see that, but you seem out of sorts. Did something happen?"

Emmeline let out a breath that started angry and became more like a sob.

"Emmy?" her sister-in-law asked in the dark quiet of the carriage.

Emmeline's shoulders slumped, and she leaned against the wall, feeling the little jolts and rattling of the carriage as it went over cobblestones and drove against potholes in the city street. Where to begin? With the return of Nicholas or what she'd interrupted?

She sighed. "I saw him."

"Who?" Charlotte asked.

"Mr. Whittaker. Kissing another woman."

"What?" Charlotte's voice was shocked.

Emmeline glanced at her relation, seeing the moonlight play shadows over her shocked features. Charlotte's reaction was genuine. "It's true. They were kissing. In the corridor. I interrupted them."

"Who was he kissing?"

Emmeline looked away. "Mrs. Bryant."

"Maybe it was just a friendly peck on the cheek, between friends. Or they were saying farewell," Charlotte said, ever the optimist.

Emmeline shook her head, remembering they sat in darkness. "No, Charlotte. This wasn't that. It was…"

Heated. There was passion there. Whatever relationship they had, she recognized it now. She'd believed in a fantasy that never existed. "I've been such a fool."

"What do you mean?" Charlotte asked.

She'd started to think he liked her. Started to think he might even have feelings for her. What a good actor he was. It was all a lie. And she'd been a captive audience.

"Nothing. I think I shall leave Mr. Whittaker to his woman of choice."

"Nonsense, Emmeline, you're always thinking the worst of people. It might have been harmless, for all you know. I shall speak with Mrs. Bryant tomorrow and delicately broach the subject."

Emmeline snorted softly. She cared for her sister-in-law, but did not imagine subtlety to be one of her stronger points.

"I'm sure it's all just one big misunderstanding."

Emmeline wasn't so sure. She knew what she'd seen. Their arms wrapped around each other with an easy familiarity that suggested they knew each other very well.

"Do you really think they could be lovers?"

"I'm sure of it. The way they held one another… It left me with no doubt."

"Oh," Charlotte murmured, then tutted. She did love a bit of drama. "Right, well, never mind. I'll get to the bottom of this. I have no doubt Mr. Whittaker will be back begging for your forgiveness."

Emmeline frowned. "There is nothing to forgive."

"But if he was deceiving you, then that's not right."

"We are courting, but there was no promise of exclusivity. He may court and kiss whomever he wants." *No matter how much it pains me to see*, she thought.

They traveled in the dark, and Emmeline tried to change the subject. "I'm sorry we left early."

"I'm not. I like the theater, but the crowd was very loud. I couldn't hear much of the show," Charlotte said.

"I'm sorry. I'd hoped you would have the chance to meet new people."

"What for? I have all the society I need, here with you."

"Charlotte..." Emmeline started.

Her sister-in-law gasped. "My God. I forgot. What is wrong with me? Do you realize what tomorrow is?"

"No. What?"

"How could we forget? It's the anniversary of Anthony's death," Charlotte said, her voice weak. "I'll spend the day with him. You should, too."

Emmeline frowned. It was a workday. "Charlotte, I need to run the shop."

"But it's Anthony's..." She stopped.

Emmeline could feel her disapproval from five feet away. "We could use the money."

"No, you only say that because you don't want to spend time at his gravesite. I understand you are squeamish, but that is no reason to ignore your duty. As his sister, it falls to you and me to honor his memory."

Emmeline let out a small sigh. Charlotte tutted. "Do not sigh at me, Emmeline. You've clearly got your mind on other things besides your dearly departed brother." Her mouth thinned into a firm line. "I only went with you tonight to chaperone you as you carry on with a man who apparently does not *actually* like you."

"Charlotte, I..."

"You said it yourself; you walked in on him kissing another woman. An honest man does not take one woman to dinner and then kiss another. If he really liked you, it is you he would kiss, not anyone else. Take it from me. But then, we both know you do not have the best judgement when it comes to men."

"That is unfair."

"Perhaps. But I think you need a lesson in priorities. Stop running around and settle down with someone who really appreciates you. Your attempts to throw me into society, even just as your chaperone, are unappreciated and unwanted."

"It's been five years, Charlotte. I loved my brother, but I have to move on, and I want you to, too. You're still wearing your black mourning clothes, for goodness' sake. You've mourned him for five years now," Emmeline said.

"And that's not enough. Sometimes five years is not enough time to grieve for someone you truly loved," Charlotte snapped. "Do not push me to end my grieving, and I will not ask you why you hardly grieve at all, especially when we pulled you out of such desperate circumstances."

The carriage pulled up outside their townhouse and Charlotte stalked out, opening the front door, and stomping inside. She didn't speak another word to Emmeline for the rest of the evening, and after a late glass of port wine, went straight to bed.

The next day, Emmeline found her black mourning dress that had hung abandoned in her closet. She dusted it off and put it on, feeling the stiff black folds cling to her soft form, enveloping her body as she pulled it over her stays, petticoat, and stockings. She pulled on a set of black gloves, tied on a set of black, shined boots and a walking coat, along with a black velvet reticule and a smart black top hat and veil to match. The effect was stark and pretty enough, and she felt the setting was right, considering the very gray day.

When she went downstairs, Charlotte had already gone. Emmeline took a carriage into town on an errand, then on to Bunhill Fields burial ground. She tried to avoid puddles and hefted a basket by her shoulder as she walked. People looked at her curiously and kept their distance, and she pulled the semi-transparent veil over her face for a semblance of privacy. She did not want to be seen and knew she was, but she wanted to be left alone.

She found Charlotte sitting on the grass, alone, before Anthony's headstone. It was small and ordinary, a plain granite headstone that bore his name and the dates of his life.

Loving husband, taken from us too soon, read the epitaph.

She stood behind Charlotte for a few minutes, hearing the birds sing and the wind whisper through the trees as the skies grew increasingly dark. She set down her basket and pulled out a blanket for them both to sit on.

Charlotte looked at her in surprise.

"You never remember to bring anything," Emmeline said, motioning her to move back as she laid out the coach blanket on the grass for them to sit.

Charlotte sat, not saying anything. She watched as Emmeline nodded to the gravestone, then sat, and reaching into her basket, pulled out a small bouquet of flowers that she lay at the foot of the headstone.

She then removed a baton of bread, and a small cut triangle of cheese, and passed them to Charlotte, whose stomach growled. Emmeline tore off a hunk of the bread and cut a slice of cheese, waving them with a smile at her sister-in-law.

After a minute Charlotte pulled back the veil over her face and accepted the bread and cheese gratefully, chewing. "I didn't think you'd come."

"I'm here."

They did not speak for a time, each with their own thoughts about Emmeline's dead brother and Charlotte's husband, gone from this life forever. After a quarter hour, Emmeline rose, dusted crumbs from her coat and dress, and said, "I'm going to open the shop. I think it's something I can do that's useful. And... I want to be useful. Especially on a day like today."

"Do what you think is right, Emmeline," Charlotte said.

"I'll see you at home for dinner."

"Wait," Charlotte said. "Take these." She tore off her gloves and handed them to Emmeline.

"What are you doing?"

Her voice shook. "I never told you this. I've never spoken a word of this to anyone. But when Anthony died, he was on a stupid errand for me. To get me these gloves." Charlotte looked at the gray, crushed velvet gloves, her face wretched with emotion and pain. "I've worn them every year since, whenever I come here and whenever I want to feel close to him. Sometimes I lay them on his pillow at night." She sniffed. "But they're getting threadbare. Can you... fix them?"

"Yes. Of course." Emmeline took them, folded them, and glanced at Charlotte's bare hands. She would be cold without them, especially in the chilly October air. "Don't you want to come back with me?"

"Later." Charlotte waved a hand goodbye.

Emmeline left her the basket, bread, and cheese, suspecting she'd be hungry again later. She left Charlotte to her grief, feeling better for having made an appearance, however brief.

That day she took a hackney carriage to New Bond Street and opened the shop. She removed her mourning hat and veil, hung up her coat, and set Charlotte's gloves to one side on her worktable.

But outside, she saw a familiar figure across the street. Peering through the window, she spied Logan Bryant talking with who else but Nicholas, which made her freeze. She gripped the small display table and when it trembled, she let go and instead rubbed her arms. She felt a chill, but not from the wet weather outside.

Nicholas looked different. He had aged, and gone was the shy, quiet young man with the mop of blond hair and rough workman's clothes she'd fallen for once upon a time. He now moved and spoke with confidence, and his soft boyish features had hardened into a solid jawline, unfriendly eyes, and a stiff upper lip with a mustache. His clothes had improved in quality, but he still talked expressively, and Mr. Bryant stood, nodding at something he said. Whatever it was, he was up to no good.

He looked up and saw her, and she turned away. At that moment, it began to rain outside, and the shop soon filled with potential customers looking to wait out the storm. That served her well, for she sold a number of umbrellas and parasols, hats, and gloves.

But then a familiar solid figure stood before her. "Hello, Emmy."

Emmeline looked up. Her breath felt caught in a vice, laced as tightly as her stays. "Hello, Mr. Runcorn."

He took off his wet hat, which was dripping, and set it on the worktable between them. Raindrops splattered on the fine wooden table, disturbing the finish. His blue eyes were bright. "No need for such niceties, Emmy. Not when we know each other so well."

She saw a female customer's eyes widen behind him at the comment, and she turned to whisper to a friend. They looked at her and whispered more behind their hands. Emmeline felt a small wave of embarrassment come over her. "What can I do for you, Mr. Runcorn?"

"Playing it like that, eh? Fine. I just wanted to tell you that I'm here in town, and... I wondered if you had any banknotes you could spare."

His skin was tanned and his eyes clear. He was still handsome, which annoyed her and plucked at her heart strings. Bad men shouldn't be allowed to look so good. She felt her heart betray her a little, and she felt disgusted that a part of her found him attractive still.

She shook her head.

"Now, that's a shame, as you've got a nice little shop here. You must take home a tidy amount. But so much money in the hands of a woman is never a good thing. Tell you what. I'll take home some of the earnings. As protection, in case any man tries to come in on your business."

"We are fine," she croaked.

He knocked a display over, sending sets of gloves crashing to the floor. "Uh-oh. So clumsy. I'd hate for something to happen to you, or your shop. All I'm asking is for a banknote, Emmy. Otherwise the other shopkeepers might be interested to know about our past relationship back in Bedford. Don't you think they would find it interesting to know who they're sharing the street with?"

Her eyes widened. As she opened her mouth to speak, he talked over her. "I'm a member of the watch, you know, one of Magistrate Tomlinson's right-hand men. My uncle went to university with him and they're old mates, so he got me a position. Now Tomlinson trusts me to look after the lords and ladies of this town, especially when he knows I'm in with the toffs of the *ton*."

She sniffed. He always did have a way with words. Lies, especially.

"We don't have anything." Her voice quailed.

"Don't lie to me, Emmy. I know you."

She shook her head, her soft wisps of hair swinging around her face. "I'm not paying you."

He sniffed and spat on the floor. "Your loss. I could make it hard for you, you know." He pressed down on the worktable, leaning over it, his cloak dripping dirty rainwater on the wood finish.

She stepped back, and he said with a grin, "I've just come from meeting Mr. Bryant. Seems someone's been causing little accidents. He's had a few mishaps. The magistrate wants me to investigate. You wouldn't happen to know anything about that, would you?"

Emmeline shook her head.

"Very well. I'll be watching you, Emmy. Just wanted you to know I'll be around. I bet we'll be seeing a lot more of each other in the days to come."

She hit the wall behind her. She hadn't even realized she'd been backing away. She bumped into a wall of hats and ribbons and knocked some over. She bent immediately and began picking them up. Her hands full of ribbons and spools, she stood to find him watching her, his eyes cold. His grin was not. It leered, and made her feel glad her hands were full, so he could not see her shaking.

He took his hat and plopped it on his head, still smiling as his gaze traveled down her body. "So much black. You look too pale. And you should smile more, Emmy. You'll put a man off if you're frowning all the time. You're getting on in years, so you should take my advice." He left, and the people in the shop gave him a wide berth.

As the doorbell rang to signal his exit, Emmeline leaned back against the wall and let out a small sigh of relief. She set the ribbons down and cleaned the worktable, scrubbing hard to clear the stains he'd left and the spittle on the floor.

She felt annoyed that he was so attractive still, and that from the moment he'd faced her, she felt speechless. Like her tongue was made of lead. She couldn't find her words; she could barely speak. She didn't trust herself, or anything she might say. She only wanted him gone.

That afternoon passed quickly, until the bell signaled the arrival of none other than Lucinda Bryant, who smiled and chatted on Charlotte's arm. Emmeline's eyes widened to see them together.

"Hello, Miss Harcourt," Lucinda said. "I've just been keeping your lovely sister-in-law company."

"It was so good of you to offer me your umbrella in the rain, Mrs. Bryant," Charlotte said.

"Oh, it was nothing. What is that between friends? And call me Lucinda, please. Everyone does." She smiled toward Emmeline. "But on such a dour day as this, I need a bit of cheer. I want to buy a hat for a friend of mine. What do you have?"

Emmeline led her to a display of fine turbans and straw hats, at which Mrs. Bryant shook her head, her auburn curls swinging around her face. "No, no, those won't do at all. I want to buy a hat for a particular friend of mine. A close friend."

Emmeline looked at her in confusion.

Lucinda let out a small noise of exasperation and whispered in her ear, "A *male* friend."

"Oh." Emmeline jumped, earning a wicked smile from Lucinda. "I see. A hat for Mr. Bryant." She looked around the shop. "I don't make hats for men, unfortunately. But we do sell some nice scarves and cravats." She led Lucinda over to the stands. The cravats were mostly pearly white with different lengths and cuts, whereas the scarves were more colorful and detailed.

"This one. This will do nicely," Lucinda said, pulling a blue silk cravat off of a display and handing it to her. "I want this one."

"Very good. An excellent choice," Emmeline mumbled, taking it to the till.

"You know, you haven't said anything about the other night. I believe you found Mr. Whittaker giving me a friendly kiss. I hope you weren't bothered by what you saw," Lucinda said, playing with a fan on one of the displays.

"Not at all."

Lucinda watched as Emmeline wrapped the cravat in fine tissue paper. She held out a bank note and when Emmeline reached for it, Lucinda gripped it and refused to let go. "It's for a man close to my heart. Such a dear man."

Emmeline offered a polite smile as she took the note and passed the delicate parcel to her. "Here you go. Is there anything else I might tempt you with?"

Lucinda's smile turned wicked again. "Not from here. Pray, what are those ugly things?" she pointed at Charlotte's aged gray gloves.

"A family keepsake. I'm mending them," Emmeline said.

"Better to throw them in the river, they're so threadbare. They look like they've been eaten by rats. Ugh. And such a ghastly gray color, too." Lucinda gave a grand shudder and turned. "Come, Charlotte, I need you. I simply must have your company over macarons at Reed's."

"Reed's? But that is so exclusive," Charlotte said.

"I know," Lucinda said, with a smile. "I'm a regular patron of theirs. They always save the best table for me and whoever I choose to bring. Come along. You simply must try their lemon and almond macarons." Mrs. Bryant left, arm in arm with Charlotte, who gave Emmeline a cheerful smile.

Emmeline waved goodbye and attended to the next few customers, glad to be busy. She was glad that Charlotte wasn't alone. But she did not like them spending time together, and rather wished they wouldn't. But she decided not to mention it, for her relationship with Charlotte, especially on a day like today, was fragile. Charlotte wouldn't appreciate her commentary on who she kept company with.

At dinner, Charlotte and Emmeline dined on boiled potatoes, stewed greens, and chicken. They both wore black, not having changed for dinner. "How was the shop?" Charlotte asked, sipping her red wine.

"Fine." Emmeline cut into her chicken. "How were the macarons?"

Charlotte set down her wine, her face flushed. "So delicious. We went to Reed's, and they recognized dear Lucinda straightaway. They sat us at their best table, right by the window, and gave us the most delicious green tea and macarons. You haven't lived until you try one."

Emmeline smiled. "And how is Mrs. Bryant?"

"Lucinda is lovely. Wonderful company. She told me about all the shows she's been in and the people she's seen. She's met opera singers, musicians, some of the great actors of our age. It's incredible."

Emmeline smiled and bit into her chicken. "That's nice. A new constable came by the shop, asking questions about Mr. Bryant."

"Oh?"

"He—"

"Between us, do you think the Bryants have a happy marriage?" Charlotte asked.

"I don't know."

"They don't seem very happy to me, but then, I suppose I feel sorry for her. To be trapped in an unhappy relationship would be terrible. I can't relate. What do you think?" she babbled.

"She seems like a good friend."

"She is." Charlotte smiled happily and drank more wine. "We are already good confidantes. It's like I've known her for years."

Emmeline disliked their friendship even more, now. She felt Mrs. Bryant was being dishonest and using Charlotte to benefit her own ego.

"But... I've heard some disturbing news about Mr. Whittaker. Lucinda told me all about him. Perhaps you should stay away from him."

"Why?" The hairs on the back of her neck began to stand on end.

"Well, first of all, he didn't call today, did he?"

"I don't think so. But I wasn't at home. I spent the day at the shop." Seeing Charlotte's eager expression, she asked, "What did you hear?"

Charlotte's eyes lit up with the thrill of relaying gossip. "They used to have a relationship."

"What?" Her worst fears were revealed. So it *wasn't* just an off-hand kiss. Not just a simple peck on the cheek between old friends, or distant family. It was real. Had they been carrying on all this time, when she and Mr. Whittaker were pretending to be together?

Charlotte sipped her wine. "Apparently, she was a star on the stage when he fell in love with her at one of her shows and became her patron. He threw money at her and practically haunted the theater. Apparently, he…" She looked away.

"He what?"

"He deflowered her. Took her maidenhood. She thought, like any young woman would, that it meant they were about to get engaged. Married. Everything was set for a match between them. But then he threw her over on their wedding day."

Emmeline stared at her. "He left her at the altar?"

"He never even showed. She was there with all their friends and family, and he didn't turn up. Can you believe it?"

"No, I can't."

"Well, it's true, he did." Charlotte sipped her wine quickly and set it back on the table, helping herself to more. "It was his good friend, Mr. Bryant, who picked up the pieces and married her himself. Apparently, he'd always loved her but never told her, since he didn't want to get in the way of Mr. Whittaker's courtship of her. She never knew. But then he comforted her after the mess of their wedding, and one thing led to another."

"I see." Emmeline stirred her stewed greens around on her plate.

"I know what you're thinking, Emmeline. And it's no use. You're wrong about Mr. Whittaker. Lucinda Bryant is a trustworthy source, and I believe her."

"But at the Lyon's Den, she and Mr. Bryant were harsh toward Mr. Whittaker, when he did nothing to earn their ire or antagonism. They teased him and used him as the butt of their jokes."

"What do you expect when he threw her over and left her to be humiliated at the church? Since then, they have never been on good terms. Is it any surprise they enjoy teasing him where they can? It's the only justice they can get, these little laughs. Maybe it's their way of getting even for the hurt he caused. Or perhaps they think if they can laugh together, they can become friends again."

"I don't think so. These are barbs and digs, and he's not laughing."

"Well, we'll just have to agree to disagree," Charlotte replied, and no more was said on the matter.

CHAPTER TEN

HORATIO WALKED ALONG New Bond Street, turned down the side street and checked on his tenant. He owned a flower shop on the street and had a good relationship with the proprietor, Mr. Banfield. He checked in and observed as the short man took care of customers and cared for the blooms, from the brightest sunflower to the wilted flowers.

He walked outside and blinked into the morning sun. It had been raining steadily the last few days. Now the sun had broken through the clouds and shone brightly, blinding him. He held up a hand to his eyes. When he lowered it, Lucinda stood there.

"Hello, Horatio," she said, looking charming in a brown walking cloak, matching bonnet and light brown dress and black boots. Her eyes held a glimmer of mischief.

"Mrs. Bryant." His tone was civil.

"Oh, don't be like that. You are so sour sometimes."

He frowned at her.

"Walk with me?" she said.

"I think your husband wouldn't like it."

"I think my husband wouldn't notice if I danced around naked with half the town," she said offhandedly. "He takes no notice of what I do, and when he does, he doesn't care." Her smile stiffened.

His heart went out to her, a little. "I'm sorry to hear that."

It must be painful to marry someone and throw your lot in with them, he thought, *only to have them lose interest and then not even notice you're there.*

"Oh please, don't pity me." Hurt crossed her face. "Besides, I have all the love I could ever want. He often takes another woman when it pleases him. Sometimes, he even invites me to join them. So, you see? I am not alone."

He breathed in through his nose, rather than giving voice to his distaste. "Lucinda, you shouldn't have kissed me the other night. Miss Harcourt saw and—"

"Don't be such a grump. What's a harmless kiss between friends?" she teased.

His mouth firmed into a hard line.

"You should stay away from her, anyway. It's not me you have to worry about. She isn't the meek little miss she pretends to be."

"What do you mean?" he asked.

"Aside from the fact that she is in trade, and those girls are always lifting their skirts and giving special discounts for the right customer, I have it on good authority that she caused a bit of a scandal back in Bedford."

His eyes narrowed.

"Don't pretend to be above it, Horatio, I know you love a bit of salacious gossip as much as I do," she said. "Anyway, I heard that she became very close with a stableboy or a farmhand who knew her intimately, if you take my meaning."

Horatio tensed.

"Her family was shocked, of course. Even if they are in trade. So they sent her away to London and she spends her days looking after that shop. They wanted her out of the way before rumors could circulate and ruin their reputation as well as hers."

His hands curled into fists. "You are talking about the woman I am courting. I'd like it if you kept your opinions and gossip to yourself."

"Who cares when she is nothing but a shopgirl? She is no stranger to men, or scandal. Take it from someone who cares about you, Horatio. You're better off staying away from her." Lucinda reached for his hand.

He kept it out of her reach. "Good day, Mrs. Bryant."

She caught his arm. "Horatio, wait."

"What?"

"I'm sorry."

He grunted when she put something in his hand. "What's this?" he asked.

"An apology."

He lifted the small parcel. "I... What is this?"

"It's a cravat. You always looked so distinguished whenever I saw you in one."

He handed it back to her. "I don't need this."

"Maybe not, but Miss Harcourt did say it was an excellent choice. She recommended it for you," Lucinda said.

He pulled back the delicate paper and opened it. Inside sat, lovingly wrapped, a men's blue silk cravat. He stroked the silk. "It does look nice."

"See? You should trust me on these things, Horatio. And when it comes to women. I'm never wrong." She patted his hand. "Do say you'll wear it. It would mean so much."

"She chose this for me?"

Lucinda smiled and waggled her fingers goodbye. "Wear it. Good day!"

Horatio looked down at the parcel. Miss Harcourt had chosen this for him. Maybe she didn't harbor any hard feelings about the kiss she'd seen. It was innocent, after all. He'd wear it and show it off to her.

That evening he went to the Lyon's Den, where he spotted Miss

Harcourt talking to Mrs. Dove-Lyon, dressed in her usual mourning attire, at one of the gambling tables. Lucinda stood not far away, talking to Miss Harcourt's sister-in-law. They seemed like close friends, chatting and laughing.

He walked over to where some of the gentlemen were betting on how many cherry tomatoes a man could fit into his mouth, when Logan Bryant declared, "This is dull. Let's have a real competition."

"What do you have in mind, Mr. Bryant?" said Mr. Banfield, the businessman of short stature who ran the flower shop Horatio owned. He wore a smart gray suit and crossed his arms.

"Something grand, for the more esteemed men in our community," Logan said. "You're too small-minded to appreciate it." He turned his back rudely.

Mr. Banfield's glare was murderous.

"What about something a little dangerous?" Mr. Ponsonby said, popping a cherry tomato in his mouth.

"What did you have in mind?"

"Darts?" Mr. Forrest asked.

"You know, when I was in the theater, the gentlemen liked to play a little game," Lucinda said, her voice carrying across the room.

In seconds, she had everyone's attention.

"The more discerning gentlemen could play a drinking game. It doesn't have a name. But..." She turned and spoke to a servant, who left quickly. In a moment, he returned with a tray of six drinks.

The servant set the tray down on a table and Lucinda shuffled him aside. "This game is a game of chance and deception. Whoever wants to have a go, step up."

Mr. Forrest, Mr. Banfield, and Mr. Ponsonby stepped up. Mr. Bryant unwrapped a lozenge from his pocket and popped it into his mouth. "I'll play too. Always like a good game."

"Will no one else partake? I warn you, there is an element of danger in this," Lucinda said, a sultry look in her eye at Horatio, and the blue silk cravat he wore.

Miss Harcourt caught her look and came forward. "I'll play."

"No, absolutely not," Horatio said, putting a hand on her arm. "I forbid it."

She turned, her eyes blazing. "You forbid it?"

He looked down at her. "This is a game for gentlemen, not ladies."

Her gaze fell to his cravat, and she shook off his hand like it was a snake. "You are not my father."

He frowned at her. "This is no game for you."

"You do not get to tell me what to do." Her gaze fixed on the blue silk cravat with anger.

"No indeed, and besides, this game is open to men and women. Whether they be ladies or not," Lucinda murmured with a smile.

Horatio fixed Lucinda with a glare.

"I'll do it," Miss Harcourt said.

"If you're doing it, then I'm playing too," Horatio said.

They frowned at each other.

Lucinda clapped her hands, bringing everyone's attention back to her. "The rules are simple. Everyone take a glass."

The players each took a drink.

"One of these has a little something extra. A secret ingredient," Lucinda said.

"What is it?" Mr. Ponsonby asked.

"Poison."

Mr. Ponsonby dropped his glass, spilling his drink on the floor.

"Tut, tut, Mr. Ponsonby. What a shame. You lose. But just think, that may have been the poison."

"I can't drink that. I could die," Mr. Ponsonby said.

"Don't be silly. Mrs. Dove-Lyon would never allow actual poison to be served to her guests," Lucinda said with a smile. "Now, I'm taking bets. All it is, is a mild sedative. The game is to guess who faints from drunkenness or poison first. Will it be one of the men or Miss

Harcourt?"

The servants all began accepting bets from the guests.

"Round one, drink!" Lucinda said.

The players drank. Horatio downed his drink in one go and coughed, feeling strong whiskey burn down his throat. Miss Harcourt drank hers more slowly, but coughed a lot.

"Finish your drink, dear," Lucinda said.

Miss Harcourt looked at her and finished.

People waited, but no one fainted.

"All right, fill up the glasses again," Lucinda said.

"But if one of them is poisoned, won't we know?" Mr. Forrest asked.

"That's just it. It's just a tiny drop of poison, so no one will actually get hurt. You'll just feel a little woozy. We used to do it all the time on stage, when we had to play an especially dramatic part," Lucinda said.

The glasses were refilled, and the players drank again. Mr. Banfield raised his glass to Charlotte. "Your health, madam."

Charlotte blinked and smiled at him. Horatio turned to Logan Bryant. "Aren't you going to toast your wife's health?"

"Why should I? For all I know she's the one poisoning all of us. How do we know the drinks aren't all poisoned?"

"That's for me to know and you to find out," Lucinda said sweetly. "Drink up."

The players drank, and this time both Miss Harcourt and Mr. Bryant coughed.

"Here, stop that," Horatio said, going to Miss Harcourt. "Someone get her some water."

"I'm fine," she croaked, touching her throat. "It's just the whiskey, is all."

Coughing could be heard behind them. "Well, it sounds like you're not the only one who's taking it hard," Horatio said.

The coughing grew louder. Horatio turned around.

Logan Bryant stood, coughing, and dropped his empty glass to the floor. He held onto the nearest gaming table for support, coughs wracking his stout frame, when he slipped and tumbled, falling.

"Oh, no," Lucinda said. "Looks like my husband loses as well."

A few people laughed, and the coughing continued.

"I think he might need help," Miss Harcourt said.

Mrs. Dove-Lyon touched a servant on the shoulder and sent him away. "I've called for a doctor," she said.

Logan Bryant kept coughing and tugged at his stiffly tied cravat. He made horrid, retching noises as he clawed at his throat.

"Mr. Bryant?" Charlotte asked, coming toward him.

He reached for her and stopped, pale in the face.

"There, he's had enough. That's two down, just four of you to keep playing," Lucinda said.

"Stop this at once," Mrs. Dove-Lyon said.

"What for? It's just a game," Mr. Forrest said.

"He's had enough," Miss Harcourt said, bending to Mr. Bryant on the floor.

"Oh, leave him be, dear, he'll get up when he pleases. You'll only encourage him," Lucinda said.

"He's not pleasing anyone, anymore. He's dead," Miss Harcourt said.

CHAPTER ELEVEN

EMMELINE STARED DOWN at Logan Bryant. His face was pale, his eyes were wide and bloodshot, and his tongue stuck out of his mouth in a deadly gasp, frozen in time. She shivered. The man was dead.

"Don't be silly, of course he's not dead." Lucinda shoved Miss Harcourt out of the way and bent to her husband, giving him a little shake. "Logan? Get up."

He did not move.

"Logan, stop playing around. No one's laughing." She gave him a little shove.

"Lucinda, stop." Mr. Whittaker came up to her.

"Logan, quit this. It's not funny." Lucinda slapped his cheeks.

"Lucinda," Mr. Whittaker said.

"Horatio, I don't need your help," she said.

"Lucinda…" He pulled her back.

"What?" she glared at him.

"He's gone."

"What are you talking about? He's right here. He…" She looked back at her husband. "Logan?" Her voice sounded small. "Logan?"

Mr. Whittaker pulled her away. She froze for a few seconds, staring at Logan's body, then collapsed into Mr. Whittaker's arms, sobbing into his chest. He wrapped his arms around her and looked at Mrs. Dove-Lyon, then Emmeline.

Mrs. Dove-Lyon ushered her out of the room.

Emmeline stood by as two servants picked up Mr. Bryant and carried him away. But whispers abounded as word spread. A guest, dead. From a harmless drinking game.

"I don't understand. How did he die?" Charlotte asked.

"Poison. It had to be. He must have drunk from the poisoned glass," Mr. Forrest said.

Emmeline looked for the bottle and approached the nearest servant. "Quickly, where is the bottle the whiskey was poured from?"

"In the bar." The servant led her to the back of a gaming table near where the group was drinking. He picked up a bottle of whiskey. "See?"

She opened it and sniffed. "I don't smell anything different."

Mr. Whittaker came over and smelled the contents. "I don't detect anything either."

She frowned at him and looked at the servant. "Can you collect the glasses, please, that were used in the game, and keep note of Mr. Bryant's?"

The man nodded and went to the errand.

"What are you doing?" Mr. Whittaker asked.

"What does it look like? If the whiskey wasn't poisoned, then perhaps Mr. Bryant's glass was. We'll have to see."

"Miss Harcourt, a word, if you please," he said, taking her arm and pulling her aside. He led her away from the gambling tables and outside to the balcony, where he released her arm and shut the glass door behind them.

"What?" she asked.

"What are you on about? Why are you acting so rude toward me?"

he asked.

"I should ask you the same thing. But then I suppose I should not suspect anything less, since you broke our agreement," she said.

"What are you talking about? I didn't."

"You did. I saw you. Don't you remember? You took Charlotte and me to the theater and then the first chance you get, I find you kissing another woman. Of all the women in London, it had to be her. And as if to add insult to injury, tonight you wear the cravat she chose for you. Honestly, why don't you just admit it? You're having an affair."

"Me? With her? Don't be ridiculous."

Her face turned red, and he could feel waves of annoyance roll off her. "I am not being ridiculous. What else am I to think, when I find you kissing her? And then wearing that damned cravat?" she said.

"That's what you're mad about?"

"Yes." She glared at him.

He tugged the silk cravat from his neck, his fingers fumbling to loosen the offending piece of material. He tore it and tossed it aside. "I don't care about it. I only wore it because I thought you had picked it out for me and wanted me to have it. I thought it was a sign you'd forgiven me for our little indiscretion."

"You kissing a married woman? That's a little indiscretion?" her voice rose.

"No. This is." He reached for her and pulled her into a kiss, crushing his lips to hers.

She felt molded against him and was stunned. She was being kissed. She felt his lips, hard and bruising, and her body relaxed and felt as if she might melt. He put a hand against her lower back and pulled her close, pressing her tightly against him. Her eyes fluttered closed, and she leaned into the kiss, enjoying the taste of him, the slight burn of whiskey on his tongue. She broke for air.

She staggered back, leaning against the balcony. He reached for her and pulled her close. "I would not have you fall," he said, bringing her back to safety.

She let him guide her from the railing, and instead leaned against one of the stone pillars that adjoined the outside balcony. "You... you kissed me."

He gave her a slow smile. "You kissed me back."

"I... It would have been rude not to."

"We wouldn't want that. I cannot abide rudeness." He trailed a hand down her arm.

She shivered, her heart beating fast. "No, nor I."

He reached for her, and she breathed in, when he took her hand and kissed her knuckles. "I apologize. My wits got the better of me. It won't happen again."

"I haven't forgiven you, you know," she said.

He pulled her close and drew lazy circles on her lower back, sending tingles down her spine.

She shivered again in the cold night air, and he said, "I haven't forgiven you for not forgiving me."

"Me? I've done nothing that needs forgiveness. You were the one kissing the other woman."

"Correction. She kissed me. I did not kiss her back. What you saw was her crossing the boundaries of propriety," he said. "Her attentions were not wanted, nor encouraged."

She breathed in the scent of his cologne. He smelled of whiskey, wood smoke, and the night. "Truly?"

"Yes. She was an old friend, once. Now we are merely acquaintances. I am nothing but a buffoon in her eyes."

"It did not seem that way tonight," she said.

He released her and she stepped back, then he frowned and pulled her forward again, holding her hands. "What must I do to convince you I have no feelings for her? I did not break our agreement."

"I do not know. It hurt," she said.

"I've hurt you?" He released her.

"No, not that. I mean, seeing you two together. And then having to help her choose a cravat, which she said was a gift for a man close to her heart. I thought she meant her husband. But when I saw you wearing it—"

"You thought it was a sign we were together, and bearing proof of our affair." He shook his head and ran a hand through his tousled hair. "She is a trickster, that woman. Always playing games and stratagems."

"Then you're not? With her?"

"No," his voice was low. "I'm not." He pulled her close, bent his head and kissed her again.

She leaned into the kiss this time, her eyes closed, and allowed herself to be enveloped by his warm body. The night air was cold against her back, but with her front pressed against him, she felt very warm. A blush came to her cheeks as she felt light as air, and she loved the feel of his hard chest pressed against her softness. Her body tensed and relaxed against him, an old feeling she'd sorely missed.

She leaned back and staggered as he released her. She ached and felt sad at the sudden whisper of cool air between them.

"What is it?" he asked, his voice deep and rumbly.

"I… we can't. I can't. A man is dead. This is wrong. I'm sorry." She turned and stepped away, opening the balcony doors, and walking back into the room.

The sight made her stop in her tracks. There stood Nicholas and an older gray-haired man in uniform, in conversation with Mrs. Dove-Lyon, the servant who had poured the whiskey, and Mrs. Bryant. At her entry, Nicholas's eyes fell upon her and he spoke to Mrs. Dove-Lyon, who nodded and motioned for her to join them.

Mrs. Dove-Lyon said, "Miss Harcourt, allow me to introduce Magistrate Tomlinson, and his constable, Mr. Runcorn. They are looking into this matter."

"We are already acquainted," Emmeline said.

"Good. Now then, perhaps we might all adjourn to my private parlor, where we can discuss this in quieter circumstances." She brooked no argument and led the way, across the room and up the set of spiral stairs, through a series of rooms to a parlor.

The ladies sat; the gentlemen stood by. Emmeline barely noticed when Mr. Whittaker stuck close behind her, trailing the group. At his joining them, Nicholas said, "What is he doing here?"

"He is a close friend of mine. I need him," Lucinda said, reaching for him.

Mr. Whittaker shot Emmeline a glance and stood behind them.

Mrs. Dove-Lyon sat across from them on a pink sofa, beside Mr. Ponsonby, Mr. Forrest, and Mr. Banfield. She said, "This is terrible. Mrs. Bryant, I am sorry for your loss. I'm so sorry this has happened."

Lucinda wiped away a tear. "I cannot believe you allowed this to happen. What sort of a place is this? I thought this was a reputable gambling den."

Mrs. Dove-Lyon's nostrils flared, making her translucent veil flutter. "I am sorry, but this was a harmless game that *you* initiated, I might add."

"Where you are poisoning the guests," Lucinda snapped.

The servant cleared his throat. "Excuse me, ma'am, but there weren't no poison in the whiskey."

"What do you mean?" Mr. Ponsonby asked, chewing.

Emmeline glanced at the rotund man. He'd somehow managed to sneak a cream puff into his coat pocket and was nibbling it.

"We say there's poison, but there really isn't. Just a strong whiskey. No sedatives in our drinks. Some of the older gents have weak hearts, so we can't be taking any risk."

"I'll be the judge of that," Magistrate Tomlinson said. "Where's the glass the man drank out of? And the whiskey?"

The servant handed the whiskey to the magistrate, who opened and sniffed it. "Smells like whiskey to me, but it's strong enough it'd hide any poison."

"I do not allow poison in my den," Mrs. Dove-Lyon informed him. "Well, nothing major. Anything we stock is completely harmless, unless taken in large doses. But we are completely careful."

"And yet a man died, of poison, right downstairs. I think that rather disproves your statement, Mrs. Dove-Lyon," Magistrate Tomlinson said. He asked the servant, "Is that the glass?"

The servant handed it to him, and the magistrate held it up to the light. "It looks ordinary to me." He sniffed it, when Nicholas said, "Emmeline. Have a sniff. What do you think? You always did have a good nose for things like this."

"What is she, a bloodhound?" Magistrate Tomlinson asked, with a snort.

"She's got a good nose on her," Nicholas said. "Go on, give it a sniff."

Emmeline took the glass, conscious of the others' looks on her. She smelled it, closing her eyes to block out her other senses. "I can't smell anything but whiskey."

"But it's obvious he was poisoned. You all saw the way he was coughing and spluttering. I thought it was just an act but now..." Lucinda rubbed her arms. "I should have believed him."

Mrs. Dove-Lyon said. "But how could he have been poisoned? The only one who poured the drinks was Peter."

The servant raised his hands. "Honest to goodness, ma'am, I didn't put no poison in there. I took the glasses from the cupboard, filled 'em and handed them to Mrs. Bryant."

"Well, I didn't kill him!" Mrs. Bryant said, outraged.

"Someone did. How else did he die?" Magistrate Tomlinson asked.

"Peter, go back and fetch the cyanide from the store cupboard," Mrs. Dove-Lyon said.

Peter disappeared, and returned moments later with a mostly full bottle. Nicholas took it and held it up. "There's hardly any used."

"No, sir. We'd add maybe a drop, that's it. Nothing more. Wouldn't want to harm the guests," Peter said.

"I see." Magistrate Tomlinson pocketed the bottle. "A drop wouldn't have been enough to kill him, or anyone."

"But then, how did he die?"

"We'll have to take him to the coroner and find out." He said to Lucinda, "I'm sorry, Mrs. Bryant, but I don't have enough evidence to arrest anyone for murder."

"What? But my husband is dead."

He shook his head. "There's not enough poison missing from this bottle to kill a man, especially a man of his... importance."

Lucinda gasped. "But he's dead. And anyone here could have done it. Any one of you." She glared around the room.

Emmeline tensed when Lucinda's dark gaze fell on her, but said nothing.

"It seems like it was just a harmless accident, and yet a man is dead. I hope this will teach you to be more careful with your games, Mrs. Dove-Lyon," Magistrate Tomlinson said.

Mrs. Dove-Lyon bowed her head. "Unfortunately, Magistrate, this was not my idea. I often encourage my guests to devise little diversions of their own, but this drinking game got out of hand."

"Whose idea was it?" he asked.

Heads turned toward Lucinda, who glared at anyone who dared look at her. "So what if the game was my idea? I didn't expect anyone to die from it."

"I won't be arresting anyone tonight. You can all go," the magistrate said, signaling to Peter to open the door of the parlor.

As the group began to leave, Mrs. Dove-Lyon said, "Mrs. Bryant, if I might speak with you privately."

Emmeline followed the group out and felt a hand on her arm. She turned, thinking Mr. Whittaker had a word for her, and she said, "Yes?

Oh. Mr. Runcorn."

Nicholas's touch was warm on her wrist, and he let go. "It's a sorry business, this. I'll walk you out."

"Um, I need to find my sister-in-law," she said.

"I'll accompany you. A girl like you shouldn't be alone at a time like this," Nicholas said, touching her wrist again.

She pulled away. "I'm fine, thank you."

"Emmeline..."

She glanced at him.

"I mean to make things right between us. I promise." He held onto her wrist longer than necessary, his thumb pressing into her veins.

She blinked. Could this be the same man who had unnerved her but a day ago? Had joining the constabulary been the making of him? His jeering expression had disappeared, and now she glanced at him.

"Nicholas, I need you," the magistrate called.

A frown passed over Nicholas's face as he released her and left.

She rubbed her wrist and went back downstairs, where she soon found Charlotte.

"What happened? Everyone is talking about Mr. Bryant dying from that little game you played. Is it true? Did he really die? Do they think it's murder?" Charlotte asked.

Emmeline nodded. "Maybe. A magistrate is looking into it."

Charlotte glanced behind her shoulder. "Who is that?"

"Who?"

"The man with blond hair who keeps looking at you. I thought you and Mr. Whittaker were courting but... Oh, I don't know anymore. Who is he?"

Emmeline looked behind her and saw Mr. Whittaker and Nicholas watching her. "Oh, that's..." She swallowed. "Let's get a carriage home. There's something I need to tell you."

CHAPTER TWELVE

I N THE CARRIAGE ride home, Emmeline told her sister-in-law about Nicholas.

Charlotte gaped at her. "Then that man, that constable, is the man you got involved with back home in Bedford, the one your family pulled you away from..."

"Yes." Emmeline was glad of the darkness, so that her blush might be hidden. "And now he's here. In London. He came to the hat shop."

"Why? What does he want?"

"I'm not sure. He seemed threatening the other day. But tonight he said he wants to make things right between us, so I don't know," Emmeline said.

"What does your gut tell you?"

"That he's unchanged. That he wants something, same as always. He asked for money and became threatening, but at the Lyon's Den and in front of the others, he seemed professional and calm. Almost charming. I'm confused. I don't know. What if he has changed?"

Charlotte leaned back against the carriage seat and rested her hands in her lap. "We should be willing to forgive people for their mistakes, and give them a second chance."

Emmeline bit the inside of her cheek. "What would you have me do?"

"It's not my place to tell you what to do. But… you are still courting with Mr. Whittaker, are you not?"

"We are." Emmeline blushed at the memory of his touch. She shifted and felt a dampness between her legs where they'd pressed against each other.

"Has Mr. Runcorn expressed his wish to court you?"

"Not as such, no."

"Then there is your answer. You don't need to do anything. I still think you should keep your distance from Mr. Whittaker, but until Mr. Runcorn says he wants to court you, there's nothing you need to do." Charlotte shuddered. "It gives me a chill to think there is a murderer on the loose. And at Mrs. Dove-Lyon's party too."

"We don't know for sure he was murdered. It could have been an accident."

"Lord. Well, either way, it is a tragedy. I'll have to check on Lucinda and see how she's doing. She'll need a friend right now," Charlotte said.

The next day Emmeline went to the shop while Charlotte called on Lucinda. But when she went to mend Charlotte's gray velvet gloves, they were nowhere to be found. She emptied the cupboards, scoured her worktable, examined the shelves behind her, moved and rearranged displays, hunting. But it was no use. The gloves were gone. What to tell Charlotte?

The days passed and they paid their respects to Mrs. Bryant, who held a small but private affair for her dead husband. Lucinda looked very pale and sorrowful in her widow's black dress and veil, and their home had been opened to a selection of friends of hers from the theater and his business partners, with the coffin having pride of place in the main parlor. Lucinda bore everyone with good grace, and had the right amount of sniffles and tears to convince everyone attending that she really did love her husband. But something about her demeanor suggested to Emmeline that she was putting up a great act, and none of it was genuine.

She really is a talented actress, Emmeline thought. The parlor she stood in was very crowded, and she went into another room for a bit of air. She found the magistrate, Nicholas, Mr. Whittaker, and some of the others in a room that served as a library, however ill-used.

"Ah, Miss Harcourt. A sad day, isn't it?" Magistrate Tomlinson asked.

"Yes, sir," Emmeline said.

"You run a hat shop near New Bond Street, do you not?"

"Yes."

"And did you know the deceased well?"

"No. Not really," she said.

The magistrate had a way of talking as if it was just them in the room alone, rather than in a room full of people. "What did you think of Mr. Bryant?"

"He had a way of putting people's backs up," she said, and frowned, realizing she was speaking ill of the dead. "I'm sorry, I mean…"

"That's quite all right, Miss Harcourt. From what the others have been telling me, he was not well-liked amongst his neighbors and associates."

"No."

"What are you talking to her for? She doesn't know anything," Nicholas said.

Magistrate Tomlinson shot him a dirty look. "She was playing the drinking game when Mr. Bryant died. She also knew the man."

"So she played a game, what of it? The man died. We shouldn't be talking about this in his home. It's not right," Nicholas said.

Mr. Whittaker glanced at Emmeline. "Are you all right, Miss Harcourt?"

"I'm fine. Why?"

"I can only think that the events of the other night were in danger of overpowering you. I would have offered to see you home, but I was needed elsewhere," he said.

"It's quite all right, Charlotte and I got home safe and sound," Emmeline told him.

She met his gaze. His gray-blue eyes looked into hers and she felt something there that made her feet feel unsteady. A heat lurked behind those features of his and his eyes warned of words left unspoken. Important words too, just hanging on the tip of his tongue, locked behind his lips.

She felt heat warm her cheeks. "I must go to my sister-in-law. Excuse me."

She collected Charlotte, and went home. But it was not long before a servant announced a gentleman caller.

Emmeline put down her book and glanced at Charlotte before standing. "Magistrate Tomlinson, hello again."

He took off his hat. "Miss Harcourt, Mrs. Harcourt." He bowed to them and glanced around the small parlor. "I suppose you might tell me a bit about this sorry business with Mr. Bryant. I have taken Mrs. Bryant's account, and spoken a bit with the others, but I wonder if I might hear it from you."

"What need have you of my account when you've heard the others already? You know what happened," Emmeline said.

"Ah, but sometimes people see things differently. Five people retelling the same story will all recall different facts, and those little details matter. Indulge me." The look he gave her was of a doting grandfather, as he stroked his small gray beard and sideburns.

"Very well." She relayed her account of what happened.

"And you didn't see who poured the whiskey, or if anyone added anything?"

"I think just Peter, the servant, poured the drinks and handed them to Mrs. Bryant to pass out. She wouldn't have known if there was any poison in them, or if there was, which drink had it."

He nodded. "It's a sorry business, this. I've spoken with the other players and none of them seemed to like Mr. Bryant, but none had a reason to kill him, either. They were all business owners who had interacted with him in the past, but none had any motivation to want to do him harm. Even Mr. Banfield was very open about their antagonistic relationship, but made it clear that while the deceased often treated him with contempt, he would never have acted on any feelings of anger."

"So you just wanted to hear my point of view? You do think it is murder?" Charlotte asked.

"I have heard from the coroner. A postmortem examination revealed that the man had high traces of arsenic in his system."

"Arsenic? But that is everywhere. It is in the wallpaper paste, the chemist, even sweets," Emmeline said.

"I know. But that amount, such a large amount in his system, over time, would have had disastrous results. But never mind that. I wanted to speak with you about something else. You see, Mrs. Bryant has been in touch concerning a serious allegation regarding you."

"Me? What do you mean?"

He rubbed his right cheek, along his gray sideburn. "She has found a pair of your gloves amongst her husband's things, and thinks you may have had something to do with his accident."

"What?"

He frowned. "Do you recognize these?" He pulled from his pocket Charlotte's battered gray gloves.

"Those are mine," Charlotte said.

"What are your gloves doing in his possession?" Magistrate Tomlinson asked.

"I don't know. I gave them to Emmeline to mend." Charlotte turned to Emmeline, her face pale. "Emmy?"

"I was going to mend them the other day when they went missing from our shop. Anyone could have taken them."

"Why didn't you tell me?" Charlotte asked.

"I was looking for them and hadn't found them. I didn't want to worry you right away. I'm sorry. When they went missing, I didn't know what to think," Emmeline said.

Charlotte shot her a look of hurt. "You know how much those mean to me."

"I'm sorry."

"That's not good enough." Charlotte's face was suffused with anger.

"Why would the gloves be amongst Mr. Bryant's personal effects?" he asked.

"I don't know. What is Mrs. Bryant insinuating?" Charlotte asked.

"She believes you may have been having an affair with her husband, and these gloves are proof of it. I was not going to believe it, but you did not deny they are yours, and…"

Charlotte's mouth dropped open. "Mrs. Bryant believes *I* was having an affair? She thinks I was sleeping with… No. It is a falsehood. We are friends. She would never say such a thing. Not about me."

The magistrate frowned, his eyes kind.

There was a knock at the front door, and a servant let in another caller, who came striding into the parlor. "Ladies, I've just heard the news. Mrs. Bryant is completely mistaken. Neither of the misses Harcourt are involved with Mr. Bryant." Mr. Whittaker's voice cut across the room.

Emmeline looked up. "Mr. Whittaker."

His gray-blue eyes sought hers. "Miss Harcourt. Magistrate, whatever Mrs. Bryant is saying about these women is false. Neither would do such a thing. And…" He looked at Emmeline. "Miss Harcourt and I are courting, and are very close. I trust her completely."

Emmeline's heart beat in her throat.

"How close?" Charlotte asked, her voice sharp.

Magistrate Tomlinson blinked. "I see. But that leaves the question of why *would* Mrs. Harcourt's gloves be in his office?"

"I do not know. But Miss Harcourt would not have put them there, or have anything to do with the man," Mr. Whittaker said.

"Begging your pardon, Miss Harcourt, but Mrs. Bryant did say you had come into trouble once before," the magistrate said gently.

Emmeline turned pink. "Excuse me?"

Magistrate Tomlinson put his hat on the floor and rested his palms on his knees. His trousers were dark gray and looked a bit threadbare, as if one more washing might wear them out. "She relayed a bit of your history and said how you had a developed a reputation back in Bedford, as a girl with certain loose morals."

Emmeline stood up, her eyes blazing. Her face was red. "That's not true. She doesn't know the half of it."

"Calm yourself, please, Miss Harcourt. I am only repeating what I was told," the magistrate said.

"Did she mention the part where I was once involved in a romantic relationship with your constable, Mr. Runcorn?" Emmeline asked.

His eyes widened. "You were?"

"Yes. I thought we would be married." Her voice caught, feeling old pain creep up and threaten to strangle her with emotion. "It didn't work out."

"I see." His eyes clouded and his face grew pensive.

Mr. Whittaker crossed his arms over his chest, looking at Emmeline. She bowed her head. She could not bear to see him. She didn't want him to see her like this. Her face burned with humiliation. He knew her shame. He wouldn't want her after this.

"I still don't understand," Charlotte said. "Why would Mrs. Bryant say such a thing? About me?"

"I rather think she thought they were my gloves," Emmeline said. "You two are friends, but we are not."

"But even so, to accuse my own sister-in-law of a crime, what friend does that?" Charlotte asked.

"What friend indeed," Mr. Whittaker said.

"Please accept my apology for disturbing you. I will trouble you no more." The magistrate took his hat, bowed, and left.

Charlotte sat back against the sofa, as if the life had gone out of her. "Lucinda. She must be so distraught. I knew she said Mr. Bryant had taken lovers before, but..." She glanced at Emmeline. "You didn't have anything to do with him, did you?"

"Of course not." Emmeline turned pink as she felt Mr. Whittaker's eyes on her. Her voice was thick. "I'm amazed you could even consider it."

"No, it's not that, I mean, it's just..."

"What I wonder is, how did she find out about my past in the first place?" Emmeline asked.

Charlotte turned red. "Excuse me." She quit the room.

Emmeline sat with a great sigh. She rested her hands on the sofa and looked at the floor. "I'm sorry."

"For what?" Mr. Whittaker asked.

"Dragging you into this mess. Making you suggest a fake courtship and allying yourself with me in the first place, when I have such a history. I'm sorry about all of it."

He sat beside her and took her left hand in his. "Don't be. And Charlotte doesn't mean it, either. She's just afraid and embarrassed at the idea that Mrs. Bryant isn't the friend she thought she was. It's easier for her to point fingers at you for any colorful background than look at her own flaws."

She sighed. "She's not wrong. I mean, I didn't have anything to do with Mr. Bryant, but I did with Mr. Runcorn."

"Will you tell me? Is this what you meant when we first met in the Lyon's Den, wanting to meet someone new, to get over a past mistake?"

She nodded. "Mr. Runcorn was the mistake. He and I were court-ing, for a time. Back in Bedford. I didn't know he just thought he was having a bit of fun, when I thought his attentions were serious."

He squeezed her hand. "You don't need to say any more, I under-stand."

She shook her head. "You should know the truth. I want to be honest with you." She told him most of the story, how she'd fallen for his boyish charms, only to be shocked when he'd approached her family for money. How she'd been shamed and humiliated and sent to live with her brother and his new wife in London, only to look after his widow within a few months.

"That is my story. So you see, I am not the sweet, innocent, or meek woman you would have expected," she said, "And I understand if you wish to end our business agreement."

"Miss Harcourt, I would be a fool to think you were... I don't know. Good girls are dull. Give me a girl with a colorful past and some good sense any day. I haven't cared about our business arrangement for some time. I care about you."

She snorted, then paused. "Mr. Whittaker, I know you don't want to talk about it, but would you tell me about her? Your relationship with Mrs. Bryant?"

"Why?"

"I want to know."

He sighed and looked down at her. "Are you sure?"

She nodded.

"I knew Lucinda when she was an actress on the stage. I became enamored with her, with all the naive fondness a young man might develop for a woman of her station. Clueless and completely inappro-priate. I regret it now, but we had a relationship together. I thought it was romantic, but for her it was purely physical. I never noticed that while she was sleeping with me, she was carrying on with my best friend too," he said.

"Mr. Bryant?"

"Yes. He didn't used to be the bully you met recently. He used to be kind, but something changed him. He is not the same man I called friend, once upon a time." He sniffed and said, "With Lucinda, we both fell in love with her, but their romance was secret. She abandoned me on what was to be our wedding day. I felt like such a fool. I discovered later that the two of them had run off together to get married. I felt so betrayed. I vowed never to trust anyone again. But then I met you in that shop, standing up to my old friend, despite his threats to not renew your lease. I'd not really noticed a woman after Lucinda until you were so rude to me."

She looked down. "I was so annoyed that day. It felt like you were trying to butt in and be a hero."

"And you didn't need one."

"I didn't want one. Charlotte had been through so much and Mr. Bryant was bullying her, I couldn't stand it."

He smiled. "I'm glad. It was the first time a woman had caught my attention in a while. You were fearless. You... interested me."

"Interested?"

"Captivated, more like. And now you know my history. So you see, I have been a fool in love."

"We both have," she said.

"We'll just have to trust each other. But you cannot blame me for courting you, fake or not, Miss Harcourt. A man would be a fool not to try something with you."

"Why would you say that?" she said bitterly.

"Because you are beautiful, and any man who looks at you sees it." He lifted her chin, making her look at him.

Her eyes met his. "No one's ever told me that before. Most men find me obstinate and argumentative."

"You are. But I also find you interesting."

"Just interesting?" she asked.

"Captivating." He kissed her. Lightly, slowly, and with a sweetness that took her worries away.

CHAPTER THIRTEEN

E MMELINE'S HEART FLUTTERED at his kiss, and the memory of it as he'd run his hands through her hair and tilted her chin up to kiss him back.

Mr. Whittaker did not stay long, but promised to call on her later. She stood by the window and waved goodbye as a servant delivered an invitation to come to the Lyon's Den.

She and Charlotte dressed well for the evening, but said little between them. Charlotte wore a widow's dress of black sheer material over purple, while Emmeline wore a light purple dress with gold embroidered thread and a sash about the waist, with a purple ribbon in her hair. Her hair was pinned in a small bun with wisps of hair dangling by her ears. A pretty effect, she hoped.

Mrs. Dove-Lyon welcomed them and bid them join the group in the main gambling hall. Emmeline stood by her sister-in-law and said little, spying Mrs. Bryant and Nicholas talking not far away.

"There is Mrs. Bryant," Emmeline said.

"Oh my," Charlotte said. "She must not understand the rules. A widow should wear all black, deepest black, for at least six months. Two years is most appropriate, but she could wear mauve or a deep, dark purple after six months."

What Mrs. Bryant wore was hardly suitable for a grieving widow. Her only nod to widowhood was a black shawl over a red dress with a plunging neckline. She wore a black ribbon in her hair, another around her neck, and black see-through gloves. The effect was very pretty, but sultry. This was no meek miss.

Emmeline surveyed Mrs. Bryant, who ignored her. She was instead approached by Mrs. Dove-Lyon, who said, "Miss Harcourt, I am glad you are here."

"You are? I mean, it's our pleasure."

"I'm so glad. Not many guests have come since Mr. Bryant had his accident, and so I thought a little games night might be in order. I take it you are acquainted with Mr. Runcorn?" Mrs. Dove-Lyon asked.

Emmeline looked over her shoulder to see Nicholas eyeing her. "Yes, we knew each other back in Bedfordshire."

"Wonderful. Mrs. Bryant tells me there was something of a romance between you? Something about lovers separated?" A playful smile was on her face.

"No, not exactly."

"Come, come, Miss Harcourt, there's no need to play innocent with me. Any secrets do not stay so for long. Now, I want you to enjoy yourself. This is to be a night of frivolity. And perhaps, second chances." Mrs. Dove-Lyon winked.

Charlotte said, "Enjoy the party, Emmeline."

Emmeline frowned. Charlotte had called her by her name, and not Emmy. Things were still stiff and formal between them.

Mrs. Dove-Lyon clapped her hands. "Now, I want a mix of players. For this game, there will be no drinking, only blindfolds."

Emmeline's eyebrows rose.

"Who will play? I promise you, it's a fun one," Mrs. Dove-Lyon said.

Emmeline wandered forward. "I will."

"Good."

Nicholas soon joined, as did Mrs. Bryant, who said, "I have been so lost. I need some entertainment to keep my spirits up."

Also playing were the charming, redheaded Miss Lott, who had chatted to Mr. Whittaker that first night, and the man himself. And to her surprise, Charlotte and Mr. Banfield joined the group.

Mrs. Dove-Lyon said, "For this game, the men are to be blindfolded. The servants and I will escort each man to a different hiding place around the establishment, either in here or upstairs, and the ladies playing will have to find them and steal their blindfolds. Whoever returns with a gentleman's blindfold first, wins!"

"What do we win?" Lucinda asked.

"You'll have made the acquaintance of a charming gentleman, and have the satisfaction of winning. Plus a bottle of my personal house wine, which many have said rivals any in France. Now, without further ado, gentlemen? Come accept your blindfolds."

The men lined up and were blindfolded, and the ladies politely turned their backs and accepted glasses of wine. Emmeline accepted hers and drank, feeling the liquid course down her throat. She felt warm and wondered whom she should search for.

Charlotte drank as well and said, "My goodness, what a diversion. I already feel heady from the wine."

Lucinda rolled her eyes and tossed her auburn hair back, straightening her shoulders. "Good luck, girls. Try not to get in my way."

Emmeline snorted and after five minutes, Mrs. Dove-Lyon rang a small bell. "Begin!"

Emmeline smiled as Charlotte giggled and ran after the other girls, pushing and laughing as they scrambled around the room. Emmeline laughed at the spectacle and finished her wine as she peeked in the doors of the balcony. A small man stood in the shadows.

"Charlotte!" She hissed.

"What is it?"

Emmeline waved her over, then went after her. Charlotte stood by the musicians' corner, peeking behind a curtain. "What?"

She'd not forgiven Emmeline for losing her gloves and not telling her. She'd barely spoken to her, except to snap at her. "What do you want?" Charlotte demanded.

"I think a gentleman is on the balcony. Go see."

"Why are you helping me?" she asked. "Why not look for yourself?"

"He's too short to be Mr. Whittaker. Now go, before someone else sees."

Charlotte went, and Emmeline passed by Mrs. Dove-Lyon, who whispered, "You might find what you are looking for on the third floor, dear. The first door on the right."

Emmeline disappeared through a door and walked up the spiral staircase to the third floor, where she was decidedly out of breath. She leaned against the wall to catch her breath but heard nothing, and tried the first door.

The door opened, and she stood in darkness. A man's voice said, "Close the door, Emmeline."

She closed it and walked forward. There were some fine furnishings, including a chair and writing table, a bed, and chairs, with a small side table that bore a flickering candle.

She breathed.

"Close your eyes," he said.

She closed them. She heard the man loosen his blindfold and take her in his arms. He kissed her, roughly. She jerked, and heard him laugh.

"It's been a long time, Emmeline. You've not changed a bit."

Her eyes flew open.

Nicholas grinned at her. "Found you."

She stepped back. "I'm not interested."

"Aren't you? Mrs. Dove-Lyon seemed keen to reunite us, especially when good old Mrs. Bryant and I told her of our past. That match-maker loved the idea of bringing together two lovers, so here we are."

She backed against the wall. "Stay back. I'm not interested in you."

His grin was nasty. "You say that now. I'll change your mind. Come here." He lunged just as she brought up her hands and knee in self-defense. He rammed himself against her raised knee, and collapsed to the floor. He clutched his crotch and moaned in pain.

Emmeline's heart beat faster than a bird's wings. She flung open the door and darted into the hallway, right into—"Mr. Whittaker."

He took her hands. "What happened? Are you all right?"

"Mr. Runcorn, he… I… I took a wrong turn."

His face clouded. "He didn't hurt you?"

"No. Rather the opposite. I hurt him, I'd say."

His face broke into a smile. "That's my girl. Come. I know a place we can hide." He took her hand and led her into a room down the hall, closing the door behind them.

It was of a similar makeup to the room before. He locked it secure-ly and put his hands on her arms. "Are you all right? Did he touch you?"

"He tried. He, um…" She laughed. "He met my knee."

"Your knee?"

She nodded. "When he came for me, I put up my knee and…"

Mr. Whittaker's eyes widened. "He met your knee."

She gave a little laugh, and he held up a finger to his lips for quiet. "Sssh."

They froze, listening. They heard footsteps come near. "Mr. Whit-taker, is that you?" Miss Lott called.

The steps faded.

Emmeline let out a small sigh of relief. "Safe."

"You and me both."

"You mean you aren't interested in making the better acquaint-ance of Miss Lott?"

His smile was warm, and the look in his gray-blue eyes sent a shiver down her body. "The only woman I'm interested in getting to know better is you."

She breathed in, at a loss for words. But as it turned out, she didn't need them.

He took her face in his hands and kissed her, but this was no sweet, light, innocent kiss. The time for chaste kisses was over. This was something more. Like moves in a dance, he led her back toward the bed, and they fell backward on it, laughing. They sat up, facing each other, and her heart began to pound.

She looked into his eyes, seeing them dark, and wanting. They sat close, too close for propriety, too close to be mistaken for a polite conversation. If they were discovered, her reputation would be ruined. But something about Mr. Whittaker made her trust him. He slowly let his hands linger at her waist and paused, looking at her with a silent question of consent. Was she open to his touch? Accepting of it? Or would she reject him?

She answered him with a kiss, light and fleeting. Yes. She wanted him, she craved his touch. She wanted to feel his warm hands trail along her bare skin and for him to take her in his arms. She wanted it all, propriety be damned.

Her breath hitched as he traced kisses up and down her neck. Her chest heaving, she turned her head to catch her breath, as he pulled his blindfold out of his trouser pocket. "What are you doing?" she asked.

"Playing. I've wanted to kiss you all day, and blindfolds have many uses." His smile was wicked.

"Such as?"

She watched as he kissed her on the lips, light and playful, then gently lowered her to lie on her back, deftly pinning her wrists above her head and tying them with the blindfold. She wasn't tied so tightly it hurt, but there was an even pressure.

He traced a finger down her neck, and asked, "Is this all right?"

She nodded. He kissed her neck, biting gently on the sensitive skin behind her ear, then kissed her lips again, his tongue seeking hers. Her chest rose and fell, and he carefully positioned himself to the side of the bed, next to her.

"May I?" he asked.

She gave a little nod as he kissed his way down her neck, to her small expanse of chest. He kissed the tops of her breasts and traced his hands down to her waist, where he lowered his hands to her skirts.

Something about the restriction of being tied back made it more exciting, and her nipples hardened against her stays as he slowly pulled up her skirts and petticoat to reveal her stockinged legs. He smiled as if opening a gift on Boxing Day, and gently tickled her legs, up to her thighs. He kissed her right thigh and she tensed.

"May I touch you?"

"Where?"

He nodded toward her legs. She nodded, a little unsure. It was a little scary, a little exciting, and she felt titillated and nervous. She looked him in the eye, seeing him.

"I'm not going to hurt you, Emmeline. I'd like to pleasure you. If you'll let me."

She swallowed. "Yes."

She felt a dampness between her legs, which only grew in a dull ache, a feeling of want as he slowly traced his thumb over her. She arched her back and leaned into the bed as he carefully parted her legs and slipped his thumb over her again, kneading the soft spot between her thighs.

She breathed in as he smiled and slipped a finger in her wetness, in her core, and made her gasp. He touched her, feeling the slick walls of her, and slipped inside her, touching and feeling as her breathing hitched and staggered.

He began to work a gentle rhythm over the small peak of her, and he rubbed her again and again. She luxuriated against his touch and ground herself deeper into the bed, wanting to feel him press harder against her, rougher. Her eyes were bright as she sought his gaze. "Please."

His eyes twinkled in the golden candlelight as he teased her again, touching her madly, tickling and touching until she jolted. Her back arched; her body shuddered. She clapped her hands against her mouth to keep from crying out. He laughed and teased her again and she batted his hand away. He smiled and licked his fingers. He gently pulled down her skirts and kissed her cheek as she lay there, breathless, her chest heaving.

Her lips felt rough, and tingled from being kissed, and her cheeks were flushed. She felt like she could either take a nap or run a mile. "How did you... What did you..." she asked, her eyes heavy.

He smiled. "My pleasure." He loosened the blindfold around her wrists and helped her up in a sitting position. He pulled her toward him and kissed her, stroking her back in slow lazy circles. She kissed him back, her hands weaving around him. They held each other close, until she broke off the kiss.

"What is it?" he asked.

She ran her hand through his silky dark hair. "I don't think this is what Mrs. Dove-Lyon had in mind when she set up the blindfold game."

"No?" He smiled, helping her off the bed. "Perhaps not. But I must say I'm not complaining. Do you think we won the bottle of wine?"

She shook her head. "I'll be lucky if they don't send a search party to look for us."

He laughed and helped her arrange her hair and skirts. Once they both looked presentable, he escorted her downstairs, his fingers sliding over hers as she held onto the handrail on the spiral staircase. She swallowed and moved quickly down the steps, about to re-enter the main room when he spun her back and kissed her. She smiled and walked into the room, to see the others waiting.

"Aha, there you are!" Mrs. Dove-Lyon said. "Although, I am surprised. I thought…" She looked from Emmeline and Mr. Whittaker to Mrs. Bryant and Nicholas, who stood with a pained expression on his face. "Never mind."

"Who won?" Mr. Whittaker asked from behind her.

"I did!" Charlotte said. "I found Mr. Banfield on the balcony. We won the bottle of wine!" She grinned and held up his blindfold, and the winning bottle. Mr. Banfield smiled shyly behind her.

Miss Lott pouted as she saw Mr. Whittaker and Emmeline together, but smiled at Mr. Forrest, who looked bored. Lucinda's eyes narrowed at the sight of them.

"Congratulations," Emmeline said.

At that moment, Magistrate Tomlinson entered the room, followed by a servant. His expression was grim as he marched up to Mrs. Dove-Lyon.

"Hello, Magistrate. We've had no more mishaps. You see—"

"It is business I come on, Mrs. Dove-Lyon." He turned. "Mr. Horatio Whittaker?"

"Yes?"

"You are under arrest, for the murder of Mr. Logan Bryant."

CHAPTER FOURTEEN

EMMELINE AND HORATIO stared at the magistrate. She felt him grip her hand. "You're placing me under arrest?"

Nicholas smirked. He walked forward with an oddly stiff gait, and took Horatio by the arms. "Come on."

Horatio took a fleeting look at Emmeline before he was taken away.

Emmeline watched them go. "This is horrible. It doesn't make any sense. Why would they arrest him?"

Mrs. Bryant stood next to her and sniffed. "It is terrible."

"At last, we agree on something," Emmeline said.

"Oh no, you mistake my meaning. He's the one who killed my husband," Lucinda said.

Emmeline looked at her with alarm.

"I didn't want to tell you, but Horatio and I knew each other. From before I was married. We would exchange letters of love and... well. These were of a most intimate nature."

Emmeline couldn't believe her ears. Her face warmed at the memory of what she had been doing minutes earlier, but now her skin cooled.

"He always liked to pleasure me, and I loved him for it. Our amour continued after I was married, and Logan found the letters. He was furious. So angry. I told him the relationship was entirely one-sided. I love my husband, you understand. But Horatio..." She shrugged. "He wouldn't take no for an answer. Even now, he loves me, you see. He begged me to leave Logan and come back to him, but I'm an honest woman. I would never leave my husband."

Charlotte nodded. She was caught in rapt attention, Emmeline realized. Mrs. Dove-Lyon too.

"It's why when he said he would have me back at any cost, I thought nothing of it. Logan found the letters and confronted Horatio; I'm sure he did. Then when we played the drinking game, Horatio took his chance. He must have doctored the drink or the glass, somehow, or paid a servant to."

"But no poison was found in his drink," Emmeline said.

"And my staff are above suspicion. They undergo background checks and do not accept bribes. You are mistaken, Mrs. Bryant," Mrs. Dove-Lyon added darkly.

Lucinda shrugged, as if it was no great offense to subtly accuse people of murder. "All I know is that my husband is dead, and my lover is the only one with the motivation to do it. I loved Logan. But now, thanks to Horatio, he's gone." She stifled a tearful sob. "It's all his fault. I'm glad he's behind bars. I hope he hangs!" She fled the room.

Charlotte said, "I'd better go after her. Mrs. Bryant, wait." She hurried after. Mr. Banfield looked lost as she left, glanced at the wine bottle in his hands, and watched her go.

Emmeline asked quietly, "Mrs. Dove-Lyon, what should I do?"

"Come and join me for a spot of tea. Although I think we could both use something stronger."

Emmeline followed her up to the parlor and joined her on the pink sofa for a tot of whiskey. As Mrs. Dove-Lyon put aside her veil, Emmeline sipped the amber liquid and coughed. "I don't know what to think. Mr. Whittaker would never do such a thing."

"I know," Mrs. Dove-Lyon said, setting down her own drink after a sip.

"You do?"

"Of course. I trust him, and you do too. I can see it in your eyes. But he has a history, and not a happy one. I think this must be coming back to bite him." Mrs. Dove-Lyon relayed the story of how they met, and how she found him reeling on her doorstep, years ago. "Since then he has kept himself aloof, and distant from others, especially women. I think he has problems trusting anyone again. But with you, I had hoped it would be different. You care for him, don't you?"

"I do. But…"

"You are having trouble deciding between two suitors. Is it Mr. Runcorn you are thinking of? Did he steal your heart in Bedford and now has come back to claim it?" Mrs. Dove-Lyon asked with a smile.

"Hardly," Emmeline said. Seeing her hostess's surprised expression, she asked, "What have you heard about myself and Mr. Runcorn?"

"Only that you were well acquainted in Bedford. From what my sources tell me all was set for a love match between you, but that your family did not approve of Mr. Runcorn's suit, and so refused his proposal. To separate you, they sent you away to London, and here you are."

Emmeline smiled thinly. "Your sources are half right. You might tell them this account of events instead. I was there." She took another sip of her whiskey, squared her shoulders, and said, "He courted me in private. I was very young. Too young to appreciate that what he was doing was secretive and not appropriate behavior for a young man interested in a young woman.

"I was barely out and had little idea of the proper behavior in courtship. We hear about such things from our tutors and governesses, but have no real clue as to what goes on, or what is supposed to happen. We are simply meant to find out for ourselves, and hope it turns out all right." Emmeline smiled. "That was not the case for me. My family found out about our secret romance, but not because Mr. Runcorn came to pay his addresses or propose. He came to ask for money."

Mrs. Dove-Lyon froze. "He what?"

She remembered his self-satisfied smile when his employer found them in the barn, and her embarrassment at being caught. How innocent it had all seemed, but not anymore. "Mr. Runcorn had allowed us to be found by his employer, and when the honest man reported it to my family, in order to warn them and save my reputation, Mr. Runcorn demanded money for his silence. If they did not pay, he would spread the rumors far and wide about how he'd deflowered me, and how I was no better than a... well. A girl with loose morals."

Mrs. Dove-Lyon pinched the bridge of her nose. "Good God."

"My family was shocked. I couldn't believe I'd fallen for a man, trusted him. Placed my trust in one so wrong. He didn't deflower me, but it would have been my word against his. Who would believe me when my own family didn't?" Emmeline smiled sadly. "I didn't question it when my parents sent me away. They paid the man, and I went to stay in London with my brother and his new wife, Charlotte. She and I have been looking after each other ever since he died. So there you have it. That's the real story." She took another sip of whiskey, appreciating the burn. It made her eyes water.

"My word. I am so sorry, Miss Harcourt. And to think I let him in here. I encouraged you both. I even told you which room he was in." Mrs. Dove-Lyon shook her head. "It is rare I am wrong about someone. I knew Mr. Runcorn wanted you, so thought nothing of his motivations. I assumed they were purely romantic. I cannot believe I was so wrong. And yet he came so highly recommended."

"By whom, if I might ask?"

"Why, Mrs. Bryant. She claimed to know all about your tragic romance."

"How?"

"I believe she had it on personal account from someone close to the family," Mrs. Dove-Lyon said.

Deep in thought, Emmeline called for a carriage home for herself and her sister-in-law. She needed the time to think, and appreciated the small, quiet jostling of the carriage as it moved through the London streets. But it wasn't until she and Charlotte were almost back at the townhouse did she notice that Charlotte was especially quiet. "Charlotte? Is everything all right?"

"Why would it be?" Charlotte said wretchedly.

Emmeline glanced at her. She'd never much cared for Mr. Whittaker, but didn't expect this reaction. "How is Mrs. Bryant?"

"I don't want to talk about it."

"What do you mean? Did something happen?"

Charlotte didn't speak.

"Charlotte."

"Enough. Can't you just leave things alone, for once? Stop sticking your nose in everyone's business. No one appreciates a busybody, Emmeline," Charlotte snapped, and gave her the silent treatment all the way home. Once the carriage arrived back at the townhouse, Charlotte swept up the steps, leaving the front door wide open.

Emmeline stared. Her sister-in-law was sometimes curt, but hardly peevish. She moved so fast Emmeline hardly saw her, and instead heard her quick steps up the wooden stairs, where the door to her bedroom slammed shut.

The next morning Emmeline was at breakfast, eating some toast and jam, when Charlotte came downstairs and into the room. She sat and poured herself a cup of tea.

"Emmeline." Charlotte's eyes were red, as if she'd been crying. The skin around her eyes was crinkled and dark hollows sat beneath her eyes. She was pale and met her gaze. "We need to talk." She took a deep breath and set down her teacup with a trembling hand.

Emmeline started, "Charlotte, I'm so sorry about the gloves. I searched everywhere and I couldn't find them. I was going to tell you, but then we were at the Lyon's Den and Mr. Bryant died and..."

"I don't care. That's not what I wanted to talk to you about. I mean, I'm still mad at you, but..." She gave a loud sigh. "You should know that my friendship with Mrs. Bryant is at an end."

Emmeline blinked. "Why?"

"She... I went to check on her last night, after Mr. Whittaker had been arrested. She seemed fine. More than fine, she seemed...jubilant. Triumphant, that the right man had been found. When I said what a shame it was that he was the guilty one, as you two were courting, she turned to me and... it was ugly. She demanded to know why I defended him, and you, when you were such a poor judge of character and he was rightfully hers."

"Hers? Mr. Whittaker?"

"Yes. It seemed that she cares for him, more than she let on. I think seeing you two together made her envious, and angry. When I asked her how she was mistaken in finding my gloves at her husband's office, she admitted to putting them there herself. She was so unkind. She called them ugly, and thought they belonged to you." Her voice tightened. "But when I told her no, they were mine, and they had special meaning to me, she laughed."

Emmeline and Charlotte looked at each other.

"The day your brother died, he had gone to fetch a pair of gloves for me, a set of gray velvet, as a gift. I was so keen, I wanted them straightaway. So I sent him, and he never came back." She swallowed. "When he died in the carriage accident, I found them on him. He'd gone to get those for me. If I hadn't sent him on that trip, if only he'd waited, he'd never have gotten hit by the carriage. He never would have died. It's my fault he's dead." Her voice was ragged.

Emmeline rose and walked around the dining table, putting a hand on Charlotte's back. "Don't feel that way, it's not your fault."

Charlotte snapped, her eyes blazing. "Do not tell me how to feel, Emmeline. My grief is mine and mine alone, and I will bloody well grieve if that is what I want to do. I loved Anthony, so much. Every day that goes by, my grief is a little less and I hate myself for it. So do not tell me how to feel, Emmy. My feelings are my own." Fresh tears streaked down her pale cheeks.

"I'm so sorry." Emmeline offered her a linen handkerchief from the table.

Charlotte took it and dabbed her eyes. "I never meant for him to die, Emmeline. And I never meant for you to be caught up in this." She let out a breath, glanced at the clean white china plates and bowls of fruit on the table, so cheerfully domestic, then up at Emmeline. "I'm the one who is sorry. It's my fault he's gone."

"You didn't cause the accident, Charlotte. He was in the wrong place at the wrong time. It happens."

Charlotte shook her head. "I can't stop thinking it was all my fault. I mourn and I grieve and it's never enough. I treasure those gloves. I loved your brother. I just... Other men occasionally catch my eye and I worry that if I shed my widow's clothing, I'll dishonor his memory."

"He would have wanted you to be happy, Charlotte. You're twenty-seven."

"And look at all I've done. It's my fault your name was dragged into the mud, and that you ended up a murder suspect. It's all thanks to me. I'm the one who told Lucinda Bryant about your past, about your losing your virginity to Mr. Runcorn, and being sent here in disgrace. I told her everything."

Emmeline pulled out a chair and sat next to her. "I thought as much."

"You did?"

"Mrs. Dove-Lyon said she'd heard the tale from a person closely connected to the family. As my parents are in Bedford, and I certainly never told Mrs. Bryant, the only person who could have is you. But you're wrong, I didn't lose my maidenhead to Mr. Runcorn. We were caught in a compromising position, but I rather think he intended us to be found that way. The farmer who found us in his barn was an honest man and told my family."

"Then you are a virgin."

Emmeline nodded. "It hardly matters now. No one believed me. And if they did not pay Mr. Runcorn to stay quiet, he would have spread the rumors far and wide. But worse, I believed what they all said. That I was a horrible judge of character and if it had not been for my family's swift action, my reputation would have been ruined."

"This is my fault. I should never have trusted Mrs. Bryant or treated you so harshly. It just pained me to hear her shrug off her accusation of you having an affair with her husband, and then laugh at me for my taste in gloves. She is not the warm, kind-hearted creature I thought her to be. She was simply playing a part, and now I see her for who she really is."

Emmeline patted her hand and they sat quietly together, until Emmeline had an idea.

"What is it?" Charlotte asked.

"I think I can prove that Mr. Whittaker is innocent. Come to the shop with me?"

They went to the shop, where Emmeline pulled out the cards of commissioned hats for customers. She found one she was looking for.

"What's that?" Charlotte asked. "Why have you come here for an order form for Mrs. Bryant? Who minds if she ordered a hat?"

"It's not the order I'm after, but her handwriting." Emmeline held up two forms. "I'm willing to bet that the so-called love letters exchanged between her and Mr. Whittaker after her marriage are completely one-sided."

"You mean…"

"If I can prove she's lying and that Mr. Whittaker never wrote her those letters, she won't have a case against him."

"That all depends on whether you trust him. Do you trust Mr. Whittaker?"

It called for a judgment of character. Did she trust him?

Emmeline looked Charlotte in the eye. "I do."

They called at the magistrate's office, where he stood behind a desk with Nicholas, examining some papers. The magistrate looked up as they came in. "Ah. Good afternoon, ladies."

"Magistrate Tomlinson, I wonder if we might have a moment of your time," Emmeline started.

Nicholas crossed his arms over his chest. "Don't go wasting his time, Emmeline. He's got more important things to do than listen to a bunch of womanly theories."

"This will only take a minute," Emmeline said, putting the order forms on the magistrate's desk.

"What are these?" he asked.

"Order forms for hats. In Mrs. Bryant's writing. Could you do me a favor and show me the love letters Mrs. Bryant said her husband had found? The ones that Mr. Whittaker had written her after her marriage?"

"This should be good." Nicholas smirked.

The magistrate looked at Emmeline with interest, and opened a desk drawer, where he pulled the letters from a sheaf of paper. He put them on the desk. "Have a look."

She looked and peered at both. "Sir, look at this."

Charlotte, the magistrate, and Nicholas peered at the letters. "I don't see anything," Nicholas said.

"Don't you? I am surprised. The *s*'s are quite distinct. And the way she signs, the handwriting is so large, it is the same in both." Charlotte looked up. "Magistrate, these were written by the same person."

"Then…"

"Mr. Whittaker didn't write these at all. Mrs. Bryant did," Emmeline said.

"Why would she do that?" Magistrate Tomlinson asked.

"She used to be Mr. Whittaker's lover, but he has been courting my sister-in-law," Charlotte told him. "She was envious and angry at seeing them so happy together, so she pointed the finger at her, by putting what she thought was Emmeline's gloves in her husband's possession to make it seem as if they were having an affair, and when that didn't work, she wrote the letters herself." She tutted. "What a dastardly woman. And to think, I thought she was a friend."

Emmeline snorted. "Sir? Do we have enough evidence to prove Mr. Whittaker's innocence?"

"It is."

"You can't be serious. You're going to take the word of two women, just on the basis of some handwriting? They could have written it themselves," Nicholas said.

"Why are you so keen to disbelieve them?" Magistrate Tomlinson asked.

"They're just busybodies with nothing better to do than cause trouble wherever they go. Believe me, I know Miss Harcourt very well. She's trouble," Nicholas said.

"Ah yes. I was going to do this later, but I see no reason not to do it now. Mr. Runcorn, you are dismissed from service."

"What? You're dismissing me? Why?" Nicholas demanded.

"I wrote to Miss Harcourt's family in Bedford, and to my old friend, the magistrate there. They informed me that you attempted to defile their girl Emmeline, and approached them for money in return for your silence. My friend supported this claim and said you had been the likely suspect for three other instances of girls ruined in the county. Care to explain?"

Nicholas's face turned red, and he backed up. "I... No, that is, it's just a big misunderstanding. I..." He jabbed a finger in the air at

Emmeline. "It's all her doing. She led me down the garden path, she did. It's all her fault!"

"I'll be the judge of that, I think. Dismissed, Mr. Runcorn. And if I ever see you in town again, I'm throwing you behind bars. Get out," the magistrate said.

Nicholas left quickly, shooting Emmeline a dirty look as he walked out.

The magistrate leaned back in his seat. "Well, ladies, if you were men, I'd hire you to the watch. But we cannot have ladies getting their hands dirty. I appreciate your help in this matter."

"What will become of Mr. Whittaker? And Mrs. Bryant?" Emmeline asked.

"I'll send a man to speak to the warden with orders to free him now. He'll be a free man within the hour. As for Mrs. Bryant, there's little I can do. We still don't know who killed Mr. Bryant, or how. If only we knew how he got so much arsenic into his body. Your average person might not know, but if enough is ingested, especially a lot over time, it can be highly poisonous and even kill. And if chased with alcohol, that will only speed up the process."

Charlotte said, "I might have an idea."

"Speak up. What do you know?" Magistrate Tomlinson asked.

"Well, it's just... When I called on her before, she was often in the habit of taking these tablets and lozenges, for her beauty. To maintain a pale complexion. She offered me some, but I never accepted, I'm pale enough. But she was determined, and often gave her husband some as well. He has a florid countenance, or did, and she did not like it. I think he took them to please her."

"What sort of tablets and lozenges, Mrs. Harcourt?" the magistrate asked.

"Why, arsenic ones."

CHAPTER FIFTEEN

E MMELINE WORKED IN the shop along with Charlotte, but neither seemed to accomplish much. They sold hats, and parasols, and took orders, but neither could keep her mind focused as they waited for news. The bell rang as the door opened, and in walked Mr. Banfield.

"Oh, hello," Charlotte said.

He came to her and spoke quietly, and at his words, one of her hands darted to her mouth. She nodded shyly and got her cloak and hat. She approached Emmeline at the till and said, "Mr. Banfield has asked me to join him on a walk around the park. There is no harm in that, do you think?"

"I think it would be discourteous not to say yes."

"I agree. Most rude. But… what will people think, to see us walking together? Will you not come with us?"

Emmeline shook her head. Customers were in the shop, and she did not want to close it on a whim. "I trust you. No one will think any less of you for taking a walk together."

"But the impropriety, Emmy."

Emmeline smiled at Charlotte's use of her pet name. "You are a widow. I do not think there will be any impropriety. Unless you wish to wait until the workday is done?"

"No, the park will be closed by then. I suppose I could cancel, but…"

"He is waiting, Charlotte. Go," Emmeline said, nodding hello to Mr. Banfield.

"All right. But I won't stay away long. I'll see you at home if not before." Charlotte squeezed Emmeline's hand and left. Once properly attired in her walking cloak and hat, she took Mr. Banfield's arm and began talking animatedly.

Emmeline grinned and took care of the customers, happy to have something to do.

The shop eventually emptied, and as the afternoon wore on into early evening, Emmeline began to clear the counters and displays and shut up the shop. The bell rang, signaling an arrival.

"We're just closing," Emmeline called, her back turned.

"Even to me?"

Emmeline turned. "Mr. Whittaker." She dropped the lace ribbon she held and ran toward him, enveloping him in a hug. She wrapped her arms around him and squeezed, making him go *oof*.

She laughed and looked up at him. "You're free."

"I am. Thanks to you. And from what I hear, your sister-in-law as well."

"Yes."

"The warden told me what happened. I spoke with him and the magistrate. You should know that Mrs. Bryant is dead."

"What? How?"

"Too many of those arsenic tablets. We know that Lucinda was taking them for her complexion and was giving them to her husband regularly. It wouldn't surprise me if he had alerted the authorities earlier about the little incidents he kept having. I heard him brag more than once that he was stronger than any prank a person might try to pull on him. Her little idea of the game was simply the tipping point to his death. And as Mr. Bryant was a wealthy and respected business-man, his death at a gambling den earned the attention of the local magistrate.

"Apparently, after he was dismissed, Mr. Runcorn went to warn Lucinda that the magistrate was coming, and rather than be caught and sent to jail, she swallowed numerous tablets and chased them with whiskey. They found her dead in her rooms. She even left a note. To me, saying she would die for me."

A chill went through her. "How horrible."

"It is like out of a gothic novel. It chills the blood, honestly. One good thing out of all this is that Mr. Runcorn is gone. I do not think he will darken your doorstep again." He smelled of sweat, dung, and worse, but she didn't care.

"I'm glad you're all right."

"You trusted me. You believed in me when it all seemed lost. How did you figure it out?" he asked, stroking her hair.

"I couldn't believe that you and Mrs. Bryant were still in a relation-ship after all this time. Especially not after her past behavior. I thought perhaps she wrote the letters herself, and found copies of her writing in the orders she'd placed for hats. I'm just lucky they were a match."

"If you hadn't, I'd still be in jail. And it's not lucky. You're smart. Contrary at times, but smart. I'm the lucky one." He tilted her head back and kissed her.

She smiled, feeling her heart flutter.

"Now there's just one thing to do. I say it is past time we end our little courtship."

She stared at him, her expression serious. After he'd kissed her, he was breaking up with her? Had she misjudged him?

"Mr. Whittaker?"

"None of that please, Emmeline. Marry me, and call me Horatio. Call me Mr. Whittaker. Call me whatever you like, just as long as you call me yours." He looked her in the eye and took her hands. "Will you? Marry me?"

Her eyes filled with tears. "Yes. Yes, I will."

He kissed her, and swung her in the air, laughing as he kissed her cheeks, her nose, her forehead, and lips. "Don't cry. You were all I thought of in jail. I couldn't think of anything but how to get back to you."

"Why?"

"I love you, you contrary woman. Why else do you think I wanted to court you?"

"But that was all a sham, to protect each other from unwanted attention," she said.

"At first it was. But after a while I realized I didn't want it to end. I just wanted you."

At that moment, Charlotte burst into the shop, blushing. "Emmeline, you won't believe it. Mr. Banfield has invited us to dinner. Isn't that kind? Oh. Mr. Whittaker." A slow smile came across her face. "I see I'm interrupting. Do I finally get to congratulate you on your engagement?"

"You knew I was going to ask her?" he asked.

"I only wondered what was taking you so long. Did she say yes?" Charlotte asked.

Mr. Whittaker looked at Emmeline and wrapped an arm around her. "Yes," she said.

"Then it's a time for celebration!"

That evening, Emmeline, Charlotte, Mr. Whittaker, and Mrs. Dove-Lyon dined together at Mr. Banfield's, who paid Charlotte special attention. Mr. Whittaker had gone out that same evening and purchased a ring, which now gleamed on Emmeline's left hand. She admired the pretty stone as it caught the light.

As Emmeline sat and laughed over dinner and dessert with the others, she reflected that having once been a poor judge of character did not mean that it would be always the case. People changed, and she was no longer the innocent and somewhat naive girl she had been at age seventeen. But that did not mean she had to punish herself for her past mistakes. She could learn and grow, and as she glanced at Charlotte, enjoying the newly won bottle of wine with Mr. Banfield, she reflected that sometimes a person needed to forgive themself, when no one else would. And that grieving a loved one had no time limit, and could not be rushed. Sometimes it faded but was always present, and it never meant a person was no less loved.

"What are you thinking, my sweet?" Mr. Whittaker took her right hand and kissed it.

Emmeline smiled. "Just that I firmly believe that taking a risk and believing in someone could end in hardship, or love, if a person is lucky. And thanks to the love and friendship of others, I feel very lucky indeed."

"I can drink to that." Mrs. Dove-Lyon raised her glass. "To luck in love."

"To luck in love," the others chorused. Mr. Banfield said so most loudly, giving Charlotte a shy smile.

Emmeline shared a grin with her sister-in-law. Who knew what the future would bring? But if Charlotte's mauve dress was any indication, she had not only begun to gradually end her mourning, but also to forgive herself, and that was a kindness only she could choose to accept.

The End

Historical Note

I've read that widows began wearing black after Queen Victoria started the trend in 1861 after the death of Prince Albert. However, Jane Austen wrote to her sister Cassandra in the early 1800s and said how her mother was preparing mourning clothes to be dyed black, which predates the Victorian era.

For this story I wanted a character to be dealing with grief, and for her close relation to want to snap her out of mourning, but to eventually realize that mourning doesn't follow a timeline. So often people tell me what I should and shouldn't be feeling, but emotions are a part of us, and I cannot stand it when people dictate how I should be feeling. Everyone grieves differently, and it can lead a person, like Charlotte in this instance, to snap at loved ones and behave erratically. I identified with Charlotte's character in this book a bit in that regard. I also read about arsenic, and how it was fairly common during that time period, being in wallpaper, paint, and even lozenges for fairer skin.

As in so many of the Lyon's Den world novellas, I've written my own take on the matchmaker, Mrs. Dove-Lyon. I envision her as smart, perceptive, and knowing when to get involved and when to leave a couple to their own devices. But I am also a mystery writer, and so could not take a pen to the Lyon's Den world without adding a dash of mystery for the characters to solve. I hope you enjoy reading. Do let me know what you think.

Acknowledgments

Thank you to Dr. Claire Sewell for inspiring me to write a charming character from Bedford. Big thanks also to my drummer, Adam, for suggesting the excellent name Horatio for my hero's character. I am grateful to my writing buddies S.E. Reed, Aviva Orr, Melanie Savransky, Theresa Greene, and Rachel Ann Smith for keeping me motivated, as well as my exceptional editor Amelia for her hard work, and the team at Dragonblade for being wonderful to work with. And lastly thank you to my lovely readers, who keep reading and inspiring me to want to keep writing, and developing my craft. I hope this story entertains and amuses.

About the Author

E. L. Johnson writes historical mysteries. A Boston native, she gave up clam chowder and lobster rolls for tea and scones when she moved across the pond to London, where she studied medieval magic at UCL and medieval remedies at Birkbeck College. Now based in Hertfordshire, she is a member of the Hertford Writers' Circle and the founder of the London Seasonal Book Club.

When not writing, Erin spends her days working as a press officer for a royal charity and her evenings as the lead singer of the gothic progressive metal band, Orpheum. She is also an avid Jane Austen fan and has a growing collection of period drama films.

Connect with her on Twitter at twitter.com/ELJohnson888 or on Instagram at instagram.com/ejgoth.

Printed in Great Britain
by Amazon

40684168R00096